The Eighth Year

A Vital Problem of Married Life

Philip Gibbs

Alpha Editions

This edition published in 2021

ISBN : 9789354593185

Design and Setting By
Alpha Editions
www.alphaedis.com
Email - info@alphaedis.com

As per information held with us this book is in Public Domain.
This book is a reproduction of an important historical work. Alpha Editions
uses the best technology to reproduce historical work in the same manner
it was first published to preserve its original nature. Any marks or number
seen are left intentionally to preserve its true form.

Contents

PART I THE ARGUMENT	- 1 -
CHAPTER I	- 2 -
CHAPTER II	- 7 -
CHAPTER III	- 10 -
CHAPTER IV	- 15 -
CHAPTER V	- 18 -
CHAPTER VI	- 22 -
CHAPTER VII	- 25 -
CHAPTER VIII	- 29 -
CHAPTER IX	- 34 -
CHAPTER X	- 39 -
CHAPTER XI	- 43 -
CHAPTER XII	- 46 -
CHAPTER XIII	- 48 -
PART II A DEMONSTRATION	- 53 -
CHAPTER I	- 54 -
CHAPTER II	- 85 -
CHAPTER III	- 120 -
THE END	- 137 -

PART I
THE ARGUMENT

CHAPTER I

It was Sir Francis Jeune, afterwards Lord St. Helier, and President of the Divorce Court, who first called attention to the strange significance of the Eighth Year of married life. "The Eighth Year," he said, "is the most dangerous year in the adventure of marriage."

Afterwards, in the recent Royal Commission on Divorce, this curious fact was again alluded to in the evidence, and it has been shown by statistics of domestic tragedy, by hundreds of sordid little dramas, that at this period in the partnership of husbands and wives there comes, in many cases, a great crisis, leading often to moral disaster.

It is in the Eighth Year, or thereabouts, that there is the tug-of-war between two temperaments, mated by the law, but not mated, perhaps, in ideals, in ambitions, or in qualities of character. The man and woman pull against each other, tugging at each other's heartstrings. The Eighth Year is the fatal year, when if there is no give-and-take, no working compromise, no new pledges of loyalty and comradeship, the foundations of the home are shattered, and the hopes with which it was first built lie in ruins like a house of cards knocked down by a gust of wind.

But why the Eighth Year? Why not the twelfth, fourteenth, or eighteenth year? The answer is not to be found in any old superstition. There is nothing uncanny about the number eight. The problem is not to be shrugged off by people who despise the foolish old tradition which clings to thirteen, and imagine this to be in the same class of folly. By the law of averages and by undeniable statistics it has been proved that it brings many broken-hearted men and women to the Divorce Court. For instance, taking the annual average of divorces in England between 1904 and 1908, one finds that there were only six divorces between husbands and wives who had been married less than a year, and only eighteen divorces between those married less than two years. Between the second and the fifth years the number increases to a hundred and seventeen. Then there is a tremendous jump, and the numbers between the fifth and tenth years are two hundred and ninety-two. The period of the Eighth

Year is the most productive of divorce. The figures are more startling and more significant when they cover a longer period. But apart from statistics and apart altogether from the Divorce Court, which is only one house of trouble, by using one's own eyes in one's own circle of friends one may see that young married couples who started happily enough show signs of stress and strain as this year approaches. The fact is undeniable. What is the cause behind the fact?

There is not one cause, there are many causes, all leading up from the first day of marriage, inevitably, with the unswerving, relentless fatality of Greek Tragedy to the Eighth Year. They are causes which lie deep in the social system of our modern home life; in the little order of things prevailing, at this time, in hundreds of thousands of small households and small flats, inhabited by the middle-classes. It is mainly a middle-class problem, because the rich and the poor are, for reasons which I will show later in this argument, exempt in a large measure from the fatality of the Eighth Year. But all the influences at work among the middle-classes, in this strange age of intellectual disturbance, and of blind gropings forward to new social and moral conditions, have a close hearing upon this seeming mystery. The economic position of this class, its social ambitions, its intellectual adventures, its general education, its code of morality, its religion or lack of religion, its little conventional cults, the pressure of outside influences, thrusting inwards to the hidden life in these little homes, bringing dangerous ideas through the front doors, or through the keyholes, and all the mental and moral vibrations that are "in the air" to-day, especially in the air breathed by the middle-classes, produce—the Eighth Year.

Let us start with the first year of marriage so that we may see how the problem works out from the beginning.

Here we have, in the first year, a young man and woman who have come together, not through any overmastering force of passion, but as middle-class men and women are mostly brought together, by the accidents of juxtaposition, and by a pleasant sentiment. They met, before marriage, at tennis parties, at suburban dances, at evening At Homes. By the laws of natural selection, aided a little by anxious mothers, this young man and this young woman find out, or think they find out, that they are "suited" to each other. That is to say, the young man thrills in a pleasant way in the presence of the girl, and she sees the timidity in his eyes when she looks at him, and she knows that her laughter, the touch of her hand, the little tricks and graces she has learnt from girl-friends, or from actresses in musical comedy, or from instinct, attract him to her. She leads him on, by absurd little tiffs, artfully arranged, by a pretence of flirtation with other boys, by provocative words, by moments of tenderness changing abruptly to sham indifference, or followed by little shafts of satire which wound his pride, and sting him into desire for her. He pursues her, not knowing that he is pursued, so that they meet half-way. This affair makes him restless, ill at ease. It interrupts his work and his ambitions. Presently it becomes an obsession, and he knows that he has "fallen in love." He makes his plans accordingly.

In the middle-classes love still presupposes marriage (though the idea is not so fast-rooted as in the old days), but how the dickens is he to manage it? He is just starting his career as Something in the City, or as a solicitor, barrister, journalist, artist, doctor. His income is barely sufficient for himself, according to his way of life, which includes decent clothes, a club, a game of golf when he feels like it, a motor-cycle or a small car, a holiday abroad, theatres, a bachelor dinner now and again—the usual thing. He belongs to the younger generation, with wider interests, larger ideas, higher ambitions than those with which his father and mother started life.

He could not start on their level. Times have changed. He remembers his father's reminiscences of early struggles, of the ceaseless anxiety to make both ends meet, of the continual stinting and scraping to keep the children "decent," to provide them with a good education, to give them a fair start in life. He remembers his mother in his own childhood. She was always mending stockings. There was always a litter of needlework on the dining-room table after supper.

There were times when she "did" without a maid, and exhausted herself with domestic drudgery. There were no foreign holidays then, only a week or two at the seaside once a year. There was precious little pocket money for the boys. They were conscious of their shabby gentility, and hated it.

The modern young man looks with a kind of horror upon all this domestic squalor, as he calls it. He couldn't stand it. If marriage means that for him he will have none of it. But need it mean that? He and Winifred will scheme out their lives differently. They will leave out the baby side of the business—until they can afford to indulge in it. They will live in a little flat, and furnish it, if necessary, on the hire system. They will cut out the domestic drudgery. They will enjoy the fun of life, and shelve the responsibilities until they are able to pay for them. After all it will not be long before he is earning a good income. He has got his feet on the first rang of the ladder, and, with a little luck——

So he proposes to the girl, and she pretends to be immensely surprised, though she has been eating her heart out while he hesitated, and delayed, and pondered. They pledge each other, "till death do us part," and the girl, who has been reading a great many novels lately, is very happy because her own plot is working out according to the rules of romance.

They live in a world of romance before the marriage day. The man seems to walk on air when he crosses London Bridge on his way to the City. Or if he is a barrister he sees the beauty of his girl's face in his brief—and is in danger of losing his case. Or if a journalist he curses his irregular hours which keep him from the little house in Tulse Hill, or the flat in Hampstead, where there is a love-light in the windows. He knows the outward look of the girl, her softness, her prettiness, her shy glance when he greets her. He knows her teasing ways, her tenderness, her vivacity. Only now and then he is startled by her stupidity, or by her innocence, or by her ignorance, or—still more startling—by her superior wisdom of the ways of the world, by her shrewd little words, by a sudden revelation of knowledge about things which girls are not supposed to know.

But these things do not count. Only sentiment and romance are allowed to count. These two people who are about to start on the long road of life together are utterly blind to each other's vices or virtues. They are deeply ignorant of each other's soul. They know nothing of the real man or the real woman hidden beneath the mask of social conventions, beneath the delightful, sham of romantic affection. They know nothing of their own souls, nor of the strength that is in them to stand the test of life's realities. They know nothing of their own weakness.

So they marry.

And for the first year they are wonderfully happy. For the first year is full of excitement. They thrill to the great adventure of marriage. They are uplifted with passionate love which seems likely to last for ever. They have a thousand little interests. Even the trivialities of domesticity are immensely important. Even the little disasters of domesticity are amusing. They find a lot of laughter in life. They laugh at the absurd mistakes of the servant-maids who follow in quick succession. They laugh at their own ridiculous miscalculations with regard to the expense of house-keeping. They laugh when visitors call at awkward moments and when the dinner is spoilt by an inefficient cook. After all, the comradeship of a young man and wife is the best thing in life, and nothing else seems to matter. They are such good comrades that the husband never leaves his wife a moment in his leisure time. He takes her to the theatre with him. They spend week-ends together, far from the madding crowd. They pluck the flowers of life, hand in hand, as lovers. The first year merges into the second. Not yet do they know each other.

CHAPTER II

It is in the third and fourth year that they begin to find each other out. The bright fires of their passion have died down, burning with a fitful glow, burning low. Until then they had been lovers to each other, hidden from each other by the illusions of romantic love. It was inconceivable that the man could be anything but kind, and tender, and patient, and considerate. It was inconceivable that he could hold any but the noblest ideals, the most exalted aspirations, the most generous sentiments. He had been so wise, so witty, and so gay.

And to the man it had seemed that the woman by his side was gifted with all the virtues. At least she had been eager to please him, to satisfy his least desire, to bend to his will. She had pandered to his vanity, fed his self-conceit, listened to his opinions on all the subjects of life as though they were inspired. If he had been kept out late at work he had found her waiting for him, quick to put her arms about him, to cry out, "Oh, my poor dear, how tired you must be?" She had been grateful to him for all his little gifts, for all his words of love. And he had seen her as a beautiful thing, without flaw or blemish. He had worshipped at the foot of the pedestal on which he had placed her in his ideals.

But now both the husband and wife begin to see each other, not as lovers, but as man and woman. It is rather disturbing. It is distressing to the young wife to discover, gradually, by a series of little accidents, that this man with whom she has to live all her life is not made of different clay from other men, that he is made of the same clay. One by one all the little romantic illusions out of which she had built up the false image of him, from the heroes of sentimental fiction, from the dreams of girlhood, are stripped from him, until he stands bare before her, the natural man. She does not like the natural man at first. It is quite a long time before she can reconcile herself to the thought that she is mated to a natural man, with a touch of brutality, with little meannesses, with moods of irritability, with occasional bad tempers, when he uses bad words. She sees, too clearly for her spiritual comfort, that they are not "twin-souls." They have not been made in the same mould. His childhood was different from her childhood, his upbringing from her upbringing. She sees that in little things—mere trifles, but monstrously annoying, such as his untidy habits, the carelessness with which he flicks his cigarette ash about the carpet, the familiarity with which he speaks to the servant-maid. She begins to dislike some of his personal habits—the way in which he sneezes, his habit of shaving after breakfast instead of before breakfast, his habit of reading the newspaper at the breakfast table instead of chatting with her as he used to do about the programme for the day. In things less trivial she finds out that her first ideal of him was false. They do not think alike on the great subjects of life. He is a Radical and she is Conservative, by education and upbringing. It hurts her when he argues with revolutionary ideas which seem to her positively wicked, and subversive of all morality. He has loose views about morality in general, and is very tolerant about lapses from the old-fashioned moral code. That hurts her too—horribly. It begins to undermine the foundations of her faith in what used to seem the essential truth of things. But, above all, it hurts her to realize that she and her husband are not one, in mind and body, but utterly different, in temperament, in their outlook on life, in their fundamental principles and ideas.

On the other side the husband makes unpleasant discoveries. He finds out, with a shock, that he was utterly ignorant of the girl whom he asked to be his wife, and that this woman who sits at his breakfast-table is not the same woman as the one who dwelt in his imagination, even as the one who lived with him during the first and second year. She has lost her coyness, her little teasing ways, her girlish vivacity. She begins to surprise him by a hard common-sense, and no longer responds so easily to his old romantic moods. He can no longer be certain of her smiles and her tenderness when he speaks the old love-words. She begins to challenge his authority, not deliberately, nor openly, but by ignoring his hints, or by disregarding his advice.

She even challenges his opinions, and that is a shock to him. It is a blow to his vanity.

It takes down his self-conceit more than a peg or two, especially when he has to acknowledge, secretly, that she is in the right, as sometimes happens. He finds out faults in her now—a touch of selfishness, a trace of arrogance, an irritability of temper of which he has to be careful, especially when she is in a nervous state of health. They begin to quarrel rather frequently about absurd things, about things that do not matter a brass farthing. Some of these quarrels reach passionate heights and leave them both exhausted, wondering rather blankly what it was all about. Then the wife cries a little, and the husband kisses her.

By the end of the fourth year they know each other pretty well.

CHAPTER III

In the fifth and sixth years they have settled down to the jog-trot of the married life. Not yet do they see the shadow of the Eighth Year looming ahead. They have faced the reality of life, and knowing each other as they really are have made a working compromise. Their love has steadied down to a more even flame, and passion is almost extinguished. They have decided to play the game, according to the creed of their class, exactly as their neighbors are playing it.

It is largely a game of bluff, as it is played in thousands of small households. It is a game, also, of consequences, as I shall have to show. It consists in keeping up appearances, in going one better than one's neighbor whenever possible, and in making a claim to a higher rung of the social ladder than is justified by the husband's income and rank in life. It is the creed of snobbishness. For this creed everything is sacrificed—contentment of mind, the pleasure of life, the little children of life.

In many flats of Intellectual Mansions, and even in the small houses of the "well-to-do" suburbs, children do not enter into the scheme of things. The "babies have been left out of the business." For people who are keeping up appearances to the last penny of their income cannot afford to be burdened by babies. Besides, they interfere seriously with social ladder-climbing, drag down a married couple of the younger generation to the domestic squalor of their parents' early life. The husband cannot bear the thought that his wife should have to make beds in the morning and mend stockings in the evening, and wheel out a perambulator in the park. It is so very "low down." The husband wants to save his wife from all this domestic drudgery. He wants her to look pretty in the frocks he buys her. He wants her to wear more expensive frocks than any other woman in his circle of friends. He likes to hear his friends say, "How charming your wife looks to-night, old man!" and to hear elderly ladies say to his wife, "What a beautiful gown you are wearing, my dear!"

He is working hard now in order to furnish his wife's wardrobe—not only for her pleasure, but for his pride. After the first romance of love, ambition comes to gild reality. He is ambitious to build up a beautiful little home. The furniture with which they started married life on the hire system has been bought and paid for, and is now replaced here and there by "genuine antiques." He puts some good prints on his walls and buys some water-color sketches, and becomes in a small way a patron of the arts. It is pleasant during one of his wife's evening At Homes to take a guest on one side and say "What do you think of that? Pretty good, eh? It's an original, by Verdant Green, you know."

He has urged upon his wife the necessity of giving *recherché* little dinners, to which he can invite friends better off than himself, and distinguished guests whom he wishes to impress. As he explains to his wife, "one has to do these things." And he does them rather well, paying some attention to his wines—he keeps a good dinner claret—and to his cigars, which he buys at the stores. He also suggests to his wife that now she has an extra servant she had better establish a weekly At Home, an informal little affair, but pleasant and useful, because it shows the world, their world, that they are getting on in the social scale. Here again, distinguished visitors may be invited to "drop in." It is good for business. A pretty, well-dressed wife makes a favourable impression upon solicitors who have briefs to give away or upon wealthy clients. One must keep up appearances, and make a good show. Besides, it is pleasant to put on evening clothes after a hard day's work and to play the host. It gives a man some return for all his toil. It gives him a reason for living. And it brightens up one's home-life. "Man does not live by bread alone," he must have some cakes and ale, so to speak.

But it is expensive. As every year of marriage passes, the expenses increase, steadily, miraculously. It is difficult to account for them, but there they are, facing a man in his quarterly reckoning. And the two ends must be made to meet, by extra work, by putting one's nose down to the grindstone. The husband does not come home so soon as he used to do in the early days. But he has the satisfaction of knowing that while he is away at work his wife is keeping up his social reputation and doing all the things which a lady in her station of life is expected to do. He thanks heaven that his wife is happy.

She is not unhappy, this wife, in the fifth and sixth year of marriage. After the first romantic illusions failed her she settled down quietly enough to play the game. It is quite interesting, quite amusing. Now and again queer doubts assail her, and she has strange flutterings at the heart, and little pinpricks of conscience. It is about the question of motherhood. Perhaps it would be better for her to have a baby. However, she has threshed out the question a hundred times with her husband, and he has decided that he cannot afford a family yet, and after all the flat *is* very small. Besides, she shirks the idea herself—all the pain of it, and the trouble of it.... She thrusts down these queer doubts, does not listen to the flutterings at the heart, ignores the little pinpricks of conscience. She turns quickly to the interests of her social life and falls easily into the habit of pleasant laziness, filling her day with little futile things, which seem to satisfy her heart and brain. When her husband has gone to business she dresses herself rather elaborately for a morning stroll, manicures her nails, tries a new preparation for the complexion, alters a feather, or a flower, in one of her hats, studies herself in the glass, and is pleased with herself. It passes the time. Then she saunters forth, and goes to the shops, peering in through the great plate-glass windows at the latest display of lingerie, of evening gowns, of millinery. She fancies herself in some of the new hats from Paris. One or two of them attract her especially. She makes a mental note of them. She will ask her husband to let her buy one of them. After all Mrs. Fitzmaurice had a new hat only last week—the second in one month. She will tell him that. It will pique him, for there is a rather amusing rivalry between the Fitzmaurices and them.

So the morning passes until luncheon, when she props the morning newspaper against the water-jug, reading the titbits of news and the fashion page while she eats her meal, rather nicely cooked by the new servant, and daintily served by the little housemaid. Another hour of the day passes, and it is the afternoon.

She lies down for half an hour with the latest novel from Mudie's. It has a good plot, and is a rather exciting love-story. It brings back romance to her. For a little while she forgets the reality which she has learnt since her own romantic days. Here love is exactly what she imagined it to he, thrilling, joyous, never-changing. The hero is exactly what she imagined her husband to be—before he was her husband—strong, gentle, noble, high-souled, immensely patient. And after many little troubles, misadventures, cross-purposes, and strange happenings, marriage is the great reward, the splendid compensation. After this the hero and heroine live happily ever afterwards, till death does them part, and—there is nothing more to be said. The novel ends with the marriage bells.

She knows that her novel has not ended with the marriage bells, that, in fact, the plot is only just beginning as far as she is concerned. But she does not allow herself to think of that. She revels in romantic fiction, and reads novel after novel at the rate of three a week. Occasionally one of these novels gives her a nasty shock, for it deals with realism rather than romance, and reveals the hearts of women rather like herself, and the tragedies of women rather like herself, and the truth of things, in a cold, white light. She reads the book with burning eyes. It makes her pulse beat. It seems rather a wicked book, it is so horribly truthful, not covering even the nakedness of facts with a decent layer of sentiment, but exposing them brutally, with a terrible candor. She hates the book. It makes her think of things she has tried to forget. It revives those queer doubts, and makes her conscience prick again. She is glad when she has sent it back to the library and taken out another novel, of the harmless kind, in the old style. She lulls her conscience to sleep by the dear old love-stories, or by the musical comedies and the costume-plays to which she goes with one of her girl-friends on Wednesday or Saturday matinées.

She goes to the theatre a good deal now, because she is living more independently of her husband. That is to say she no longer waits for his home-coming, as in her first days of marriage, with an impatient desire. She has long seen that they cannot be all in all to each other, sharing all pleasures, or having none. He has realized that, too, and goes to his club at least once a week—sometimes more often, to enjoy the society of men, to get a little "Bohemianism," as he calls it.

She has made her own circle of friends now, the young wives of men like her husband, and many of her afternoons are taken up with little rounds of visits, when she is amused by the tittle-tattle of these wives, by their little tales and scandals, by their gossips about servants, frocks and theatres.

She, too, has social ambitions like her husband. Her evenings At Home are agreeable adventures when she is pleased with the homage of her husband's friends. She takes some trouble with her little dinner-parties and writes out the *menus* with a good deal of care, and arranges the flowers, and occasionally looks into the kitchen to give a word to the cook. She wears her new evening gown and smiles at her husband's compliments, with something of her old tenderness. After one of these evening At Homes the husband and wife have moments of loving comradeship like those in the first days of their marriage. It is a pity that some trivial accident or dispute causes ill-temper at the breakfast-table.

But, on the whole, they play the game rather well in the fifth and sixth years of their married life. The husband takes the rough with the smooth. In spite of occasional bad tempers, in spite of grievances which are growing into habits of mind, he is a good fellow and—he thanks heaven his wife is happy.

CHAPTER IV

It is the seventh year. The wife is still doing exactly what she did in the fifth and sixth years. Her daily routine is exactly the same. Except that she can afford extra little luxuries now, and indulge in more expensive kinds of pleasure—stalls at the theatre instead of seats in the pit, an occasional visit to the opera, an easy yielding to temptations in the way of hats. Her husband has been "getting on," and he is glad to give her what she wants.

But somehow or other she is beginning to realize that she has not got what she wants. She does not know what she wants, but she knows that there is a great lack of something in her life. She is still "playing the game," but there is no longer the same sport in it. The sharp edge of her interest in things has worn off. It has been dulled down. She goes languidly through the days and a matinée jaunt no longer thrills her with a little excitement. The plays are so boring, full of stale old plots, stale old women, stale old tricks. She is sick of them. She still reads a great number of romantic novels, but how insufferably tedious they have become! How false they are! How cloying is all this sickly sentiment! She searches about for the kind of novel which used to frighten her, problem novels, dangerous novels, novels dealing with real problems of life. They still frighten her a little, some of them, but she likes the sensation. She wants more of it. She wants to plunge deeper into the dangerous problems, to get nearer to the truth of things. She broods over their revelations. She searches out the meaning of their suggestions, their hints, their innuendoes. It is like drug-drinking. This poisonous fiction stimulates her for a little while, until the effect of it has worn off and leaves her with an aching head. Her head often aches now. And her heart aches— though goodness knows why. Everything is so stale. The gossip of her women friends is, oh—so stale! She has heard all their stories about all their servants, all their philosophy about the servant problem in general, all their shallow little views about life, and love, and marriage. She has found them all out, their vanities, their little selfish ways, their little lies and shams and fooleries. They are exactly like herself. She has been brought up in the same code, shaped in the same mould, cut out to the same pattern.

Their ideas are her ideas. Their ways of life her ways. They bore her exceedingly.

She is bored by things which for a time were very pleasant. It is, for instance, boring to go shopping in the morning. It is annoying to her to see her own wistful, moody eyes in the plate-glass windows, and in the pier-glasses. She has not lost her love of pretty frocks and pretty things, but it bores her to think that her husband does not notice them so much, and that she has to wear them mostly to please herself. She is tired of the little compliments paid to her by her husband's middle-aged friends. She has begun to find her husband's friends very dull people indeed. Most of all is she bored by those evening At Homes with their familiar ritual—the girl who wants to sing but pleads a bad cold, the woman who wants to play but says she is so fearfully "out of practice," the man who asks the name of a piece which he has heard a score of times, the well-worn jokes, the well-known opinions on things which do not matter, the light refreshments, the thanks for "a pleasant evening." Oh, those pleasant evenings! How she hates them!

She is beginning to hate this beautiful little home of hers. The very pictures on the walls set her nerves on edge. She has stared at them so often. She wishes to goodness that Marcus Stone's lovers on an old-fashioned stone seat would go and drown themselves in the distant lake. But they do not move. They sit smirking at each other, eternally. She wishes with all her heart that the big Newfoundland dog over there would bite the fluffy haired child who says "Does 'oo talk?" But it will not even bark. She stares at the pattern on the carpet, when a Mudie's novel lies on her lap, and comes to detest the artificial roses on the trellis-work. She digs her heels into one of them. If the roses were real she would pluck them leaf by leaf and scatter the floor with them. The ticking of the clock on the mantelshelf irritates her. It seems a reproach to her. It seems to be counting up her waste of time.

She stays more at home, in spite of hating it, because she is beginning to loathe her round of visits. She feels lonely and wishes her husband would come home. Why does he stay so late at the office now? Surely it isn't necessary? When he comes home she is so snappy and irritable that he becomes silent over the dinner-table, and then she quarrels with him for his silence. After dinner he sits over his papers, thinking out some knotty point of business, which he does not discuss with her as in the old days. He buries his nose in the evening paper, and reads all the advertisements, and is very dull and uninteresting. Yet she nourishes a grievance when he goes off on his club-nights and comes home in the early hours of the morning, cheerful and talkative when she wants to go to sleep.

CHAPTER V

In some cases, indeed in many cases, the presence of an "outsider" adds to the unhappiness of the wife and divides her still more from her husband. It is the presence of the mother-in-law.

She, poor soul, has had a terrible time, and no one until now has said a good word for her. The red-nosed comedian of the music-hall has used her for his most gross vulgarities, sure that whenever he mentions her name he will raise guffaws from the gallery, and evoke shrieks of ill-natured merriment from young women in the pit. In the pantomimes the man dressed up as a woman indulges in long monologues upon his mother-in-law as the source of all domestic unhappiness, as the origin of all quarrels between husbands and wives, as the greatest nuisance in modern life, and so long as he patters about the mother-in-law the audience enjoys itself vastly.

It is idle to pretend that the mother-in-law is a blessing in a small household. I am bound to admit that the success of the rednosed comedian who uses her as his text is due to the truth which lies hidden beneath his absurdity. He raises roars of laughter because the people who make up his audience realize that he is giving a touch of humor to something which is a grim tragedy, and according to the psychology of humor this is irresistibly comic, just as the most primitive and laughter-compelling jokes deal with corpses, and funerals, and death made ridiculous. They have suffered from their own mothers-in-law, those elderly women who sit in the corner with watchful eyes upon the young wives, those critics of their sons' marriages, those eavesdroppers of the first quarrel, and of all the quarrels that follow the first, those oracles of unwelcome wisdom, whose advice about household affairs, about the way of dealing with the domestic servants, with constant references to *their* young days, are a daily exasperation to young married women.

All that is painfully true. In many cases the mother-in-law becomes so terrible an incubus in small households that domestic servants leave with unfailing regularity before their month is "up," husbands make a habit of being late at the office, and wives are seriously tempted to take to drink.

But what of the mother-in-law herself? Is *she* to be envied? Did she willingly become a mother-in-law? Alas, her tragedy is as great as that of the young wife upon whose nerves she gets so badly, as great as that of the young husband who finds his home-life insufferable because of her presence.

For the mother-in-law is a prisoner of fate. She is the unwanted guest. She is dependent upon the charity of those who find her a daily nuisance. During the days of her own married life she devoted herself to her husband and children, stinted and scraped for them, moulded them according to her ideals of righteousness, exacted obedience to her motherly commands, and was sure of their love. Then, one day, death knocked at the door, and brought black horses into the street. After that day, when her man was taken from her, she became dependent upon her eldest son, but did not yet feel the slavery of the dependence.

For he paid the debt of gratitude gratefully, and kept up the little home.

But one day she noticed that he did not come home so early, and that when he came home he was absent-minded. He fell into the habit of spending his evenings out, and his mother wondered, and was anxious. He was not so careful about her comforts, and she was hurt. Then one day he came home and said, "Mother, I am going to get married," and she knew that her happiness was at an end. For she knew, with a mother's intuition, that the love which had been in her boy's heart for her must now be shared with another woman, and that instead of having the first place in his life, she would have the second place.

For a little while her jealousy is like that of a woman robbed of her lover. She hides it, and hides her hate for that girl whose simpering smile, whose prettiness, whose coy behavior, light fires in her son's eyes, and set his pulse beating, and make him forgetful of his mother.

Then the marriage takes place and the mother who has dreaded the day knows that it is her funeral. For she is like a queen whose prerogatives and privileges have been taken away by the death of the king, and by the accession of a new queen. Her place is taken from her. Her home is broken up. She is moved, with the furniture, into the new home, put into the second-best bedroom, and arranged to suit the convenience of the new household in which another woman is mistress.

She knows already that she has begun to be a nuisance, and it is like a sharp dagger in her heart. She knows that the young wife is as jealous of her as she is of the young wife, because her son cannot break himself of the habit of obedience, cannot give up that respect for his mother's principles and advice and wisdom, which is part of the very fibre of his being, because in any domestic crisis the son turns more readily to the mother than to the young woman who is a newcomer in his life, and in any domestic quarrel he takes the mother's part rather than the wife's. It is the law of nature. It cannot be altered, but it is the cause of heartburning and squalid little tragedies.

The mother-in-law, in the corner of the sitting-room, watches the drama of the married life, and with more experience of life, because of her years, sees the young wife do foolish things, watches her blundering experiments in the great adventure of marriage, is vigilant of her failures in housekeeping, and in the management of her husband. She cannot be quite tongue-tied. She cannot refrain from criticism, advice, rebuke. Between the mother-in-law and the daughter-in-law there is a daily warfare of pinpricks, a feud that grows bitter with the years.

But the mother-in-law is helpless. She cannot escape from the lamentable situation. She must always remain a hindrance, because she needs a roof over her head, and there is no other roof, and she is dependent for her daily bread upon the son who is faithful to her, though he is irritable, moody and sharp of speech, because of the fretfulness of his wife.

This is the eternal tragedy of the mother-in-law, which is turned into a jest by the red-nosed comedian to get the laughter from "the gods." It is also a tragedy to the daughter-in-law, who could shriek aloud sometimes when the presence of the elderly woman becomes intolerable.

Many things are becoming intolerable to the young wife. Her nerves are out of order. Sometimes she feels "queer." She cannot explain how queer she feels, even to herself. She says bitter things to her husband, and then hates herself for doing so. She has a great yearning for his love, but is very cold when he is in a tender mood. She cannot understand her own moods. She only knows that she is beginning to get frightened when she thinks of the long vista of years before her. She cannot go on like this always. She cannot go on like this very long. She is getting rather hysterical. She startles her husband by laughing in a queer shrill way when he expresses some serious opinions, or gives vent to some of his conventional philosophy, about women, and the duties of married life, and the abomination of the Suffragettes. But he does not see her tears. He does not see her one day, when suddenly, after she has been reading a Mudie's novel, page after page, without understanding one word, tears well up into her eyes, and fall upon the pages, until she bends her head down and puts her hands up to her face, and sobs as though all her heart had turned to tears.

CHAPTER VI

It is the Eighth Year. The wife does not know the significance of that. The husband goes on his way without seeing the ghosts that have invaded his little household. He is too busy to see. The whole energy of his mind now is devoted to the business of his life. He must earn money, more money, still more money, because expenses still keep increasing, by leaps and bounds. He finds it more and more difficult to cut his coat according to his cloth. He is often surprised because with a much larger income he seems to be just as "hard up" as when he started the adventure of marriage. He wonders, sometimes, whether the game is worth the candle. What does he get out of it? Precious little. Not much fun. In the evenings he is tired, although his brain is still worrying over the details of his work, over his business disappointments and difficulties, and plans. Now and again he is surprised at the strange quietude and lassitude of his wife. He catches a look of tragedy in her eyes, and it startles him for a moment, so that he asks her if she is feeling unwell. She laughs, in a mirthless way, and seems to resent the question. "Perfectly well, thanks," she says. He shrugs his shoulders. He cannot bother about a woman's whims and moods. Women are queer kittle-cattle. He can't make 'em out. Even his own wife is a perfect mystery to him. It is a pity they get on each other's nerves so much. What more does she want? He has given her everything a woman may desire—a beautiful little home, many little luxuries, plenty of pin-money. He does not stint her. It is he that does the stinting. He is always working for her so that she may play. However—work is best. To do our job in life is the best philosophy.

So the husband has on one side the passing suspicion that something is wrong with his wife, and the wife hides her heart from him.

Something *is* wrong with her. Everything is wrong, though she does not know why and how. She feels lonely—horribly lonely in spite of all her friends. She feels like a woman alone in a great desert with no other human soul near her, thrust back upon her own thoughts, brooding over her own misery. There is a great emptiness in her heart, and she has a great hunger and a great thirst of soul which she cannot satisfy. Nothing satisfies that empty, barren heart of hers, that throbbing brain. She has finished with Mudie's novels. She can find no satisfaction in *them*. She revolts from the tittle-tattle of her women friends. That is no longer amusing. She finds no pleasure in the beauty of her face. It is no longer beautiful. She hates the sight of her face in the glass. She is afraid of those big wistful eyes which stare at her. She is sick to death of dressing herself up. How futile it is! How utterly vain and foolish!

She is haunted with ghosts; the ghosts of What-Might-Have-Been. They whisper about her, so that she puts her hands to her ears, when she is alone in her drawing-room. Faces peer at her, with mocking eyes, or with tempting eyes—the faces of men who might have been her lovers, baby faces of unborn children. Little hands flutter about her heart, pluck at her, tease her. The ghosts of her girlhood crowd about her, the ghosts of dead hopes, of young illusions, of romantic dreams. She thrusts them away from her vision. She puts her hands before her eyes, and moans a little, quietly, so that the servants in the kitchen shall not hear.

She is assailed by strange temptations, horrible temptations, from which she shrinks back afraid. This hunger and thirst in her soul are so tormenting that she has frightful cravings for Something to satisfy her hunger and quench her thirst. She is tempted to take to drink, or to drugs, to dull the throbbing of her brain, to wake her up out of this awful lassitude, to give her a momentary excitement and vitality, and then—forgetfulness. She must have some kind of excitement—to break the awful monotony of her life, this intolerable dullness of her little home. If only an adventure would come to her! Some thrilling, perilous adventure, however wicked, whatever the consequences. She feels the overmastering need of some passionate emotion. She would like to plunge into romantic love again, to be set on fire by it. Somewhere about the world is a man who could save her, some strong man with a masterful way with him, brutal as well as tender, cruel as well as kind, who would come to her, and clasp her hands, and capture her. She would lean upon him. She would yield, willingly.... She tries to crush down these thoughts. She is horrified at the evil in them. Oh, she is a bad woman! Even in her loneliness her face scorches with shame. She gives a faint cry to God to save her. But again and again the devilish thoughts leer up in her brain. She begins to believe that the devil is really busy with her and that she cannot escape him.

She has a strange sense of impending peril, of something that is going to happen. She knows that something *must* happen.

In this Eighth Year she is in a state bordering on hysteria, when anything may happen to her. Even her husband is beginning to get alarmed. He is at last awakened out of his self-complacency. He is beginning to watch her, with a vague uneasiness. Why does she look so queerly at him sometimes as though she hated him? Why does she say such bitter, cruel, satirical things, which stab him and leave a poison in the wound? Why does she get into such passionate rages about trivial things, and then reveal a passionate remorse? Why does she sink into long silences, sitting with her hands in her lap, staring at the pattern on the carpet, as though it had put a spell upon her? He cannot understand. She says there is nothing wrong with her health, she refuses to see a doctor. She scoffs at the idea of going away for a little holiday to the seaside. She says it would bore her to death. Once she bursts into tears and weeps on his shoulder. But she cannot, or will not, explain the cause of her tears, so that he becomes impatient with her and talks to her roughly, though he is sorry afterwards. He begins to see now that marriage is a difficult game. Perhaps they were not suited to each other. They married too young, before they had understood each other.... However they have got to make the best of it now. That is the law of life—to make the best of it.

So in the Eighth Year the husband tries to take a common-sense view of things, not knowing that in the Eighth Year it is too late for common sense as far as the wife is concerned. She wants uncommon sense. Only some tremendous and extraordinary influence, spiritual, or moral, or intellectual, beyond the limits of ordinary common sense, may save her from the perils in her own heart. She must find a way of escape, for these unsatisfied yearnings, for this beating heart, for this throbbing brain. Her little home has become a cage to her. Her husband has become her jailer. Her life has become too narrow, too petty, too futile. In the Eighth Year she must find a way of escape—anyhow, anywhere. And in the Eighth Year the one great question is in what direction will she go? There are many ways of escape.

CHAPTER VII

One way of escape is through the door of the Divorce Court. Sir Francis Jeune, when he was President of the Divorce Court, saw before him many of these escaping women, and he noted down the fact about the Eighth Year; and sitting there with an impassive face, but watchful eyes, he saw the characters in all these little tragedies and came to know the type and the plot from constant reiteration. Sometimes the plot varied, but only in accidentals, never in essentials. As the story was rehearsed before him, it always began in the same way, with a happy year or two of marriage. Then it was followed by the first stress and strain. Then there came the drifting apart, the little naggings, the quarrels, the misunderstandings, until the wife—it was generally the wife—became bored, lonely, emotional, hysterical, and an easy victim for the first fellow with a roving eye, a smooth tongue, and an easy conscience. The procession still goes on, the long procession of women who try to escape through the Divorce Court door. Every year they come, and the same story is told and retold with sickening repetition. In most cases they are childless wives. That is proved, beyond dispute, by all statistics of divorce. Sometimes they have one or two children, but those cases are much more rare. But even when there are children to complicate the issues and to be the heirs of these tragedies, the causes behind the tragedies are the same. The woman has had idle hands in her lap before the Eighth Year of marriage has been reached. In the early years her little home was enough to satisfy her mind and heart, and her interests were enough to keep her busy. The coming of the first child, and of the second, if there is a second, was for a time sufficient to crowd her day with little duties and to prevent any restlessness or any deadly boredom. All went well while she had but one maidservant, and while her husband's feet were still on the lower rungs of the ladder. But the trouble began with the arrival of the extra servant and with the promotion of her husband. It began when gradually she handed over domestic duties to paid people, when she was seldom in the kitchen and more in the drawing-room, when the children were put under the charge of a nurse, and when the responsibilities of motherhood had become a sinecure. The fact must be faced that a child is not always a cure for the emptiness of a woman's heart, nor an absolute pledge of fidelity between husband and wife. These women who seek a way of escape from their little homes are not always brought to that position by the unfulfilled instincts of motherhood. For many of them have no instincts of motherhood. They feel no great natural desire to have a child. They even shrink from the idea of motherhood, and plead their lack of courage, their ill-health, their weakness. With their husbands they are partners in a childless scheme, or if they have a child—they quickly thrust it into the nursery to leave themselves free.

But, on the other hand, it is a fact borne out by all the figures that a child does in the vast majority of cases bind together the husband and wife, as no other influence or moral restraint; and that among all the women who come to the Divorce Court the overwhelming majority is made up of childless wives.

These women are not naturally vicious. They have not gone wrong because their principles are perverted. They are not, as a rule, intellectual anarchists who have come to the conclusion that the conventional moral code is wrong and that the laws of marriage are neither divine nor just. On the contrary, they are conscience-stricken, they are terrified by their own act. Many of them are brokenhearted and filled with shame. It is pitiful to hear their letters read in court, letters to their husbands pleading for forgiveness, asking for "another chance," or trying, feebly, to throw the blame on the man, and to whitewash themselves as much as possible. To judge from their letters it would seem that they were under some evil spell, and that they were conscious of being dragged away from their duty as though Fate had clutched them by the hair, so that although they struggled they could not resist, and were borne helplessly along upon a swift tide of passion carrying them to destruction. "I could not help myself" is the burden of their cry, as though they had no free-will, and no strength of will. Occasionally they give tragic pictures of their idle lives, so lacking in interest, so barren, so boring. There is another phrase which crops up again and again: "Oh, I was bored—bored—bored!" It was the man that saved her from boredom who now shares the woman's guilt, and stands in the witness box in this court of honor. He came to her just at that moment in the Eighth Year when she was bored to death. He was kind, sympathetic, understanding. He brought a little color back into her cheeks, a little laughter into her eyes, a little sunshine into her life. He seemed such a boy, so youthful and high-spirited, such a contrast to her husband, always busy, and always worrying over his business. He told good stories, took her to the theatre, arranged little supper-parties, made a new adventure of life. He would sit chatting with her over the fire, when there were flickering shadows on the walls. He chased away the ghosts, gave her new dreams, brought new hopes.... And then suddenly he begins to tempt her; and she shrinks back from him, and is afraid. He knows she is afraid, but he tries to laugh away her fears. She pleads with him to go away, but there is insincerity in her voice, her words are faltering. She knows that if he were to go away she would be left more lonely than before, in intolerable loneliness till the ghosts would rush back at her. So he stays, and tempts her a little more. Gradually, little by little, he becomes her great temptation, overwhelming all other things in life dwarfing all other things, even her faith and honor. How can she resist? By what power within her can she resist?

She does not resist. And yet by yielding she does not gain that happiness to which she stretched out her hands. She does not satisfy the great hunger in her heart or quench her burning thirst. She has not even killed the ghosts which haunt her, or healed the pin pricks of her conscience. Her conscience is one great bleeding wound. For this woman of the middle-classes is a creature of her caste Nor in most cases can she break the rules of her caste without frightful hurt to herself. She was brought up in a "nice" home. Her mother was a woman of old-fashioned virtues. Her father was a man who would have seen her dead rather than shamed. She received a High School education, and read Tennyson and Longfellow with moral notes by her class-mistress. She used to go to church, and sometimes goes there still, though without any fervor or strength of faith. She has heard the old words, "The wages of sin is death," and she shrinks a little when she thinks of them. Above all she has been brought up on romantic fiction, and that is always on the side of the angels. The modern problem novel has arrested her intellect, has startled her, challenged her, given her "notions"; but in her heart of hearts she still believes in the old-fashioned code of morals, in the sweet old virtues. This sin of hers is a great terror to her. She is not brazen-faced. She does not justify it by any advanced philosophy. She is just a poor, weak, silly woman, who has gone to the edge of a precipice, grown giddy, and fallen off the cliff. She throws up her hands with a great cry. The way of escape through the Divorce Court door is not a way to happiness. It is a way to remorse, to secret agonies, to a life-long wretchedness. Her second husband, if he "plays the game" according to the rules of the world, is not to be envied. Between him and this woman there are old ghosts. This way of escape is into a haunted house.

CHAPTER VIII

Thousands, and tens of thousands of women who pass through the Eighth Year, not unscathed, find another way out. They are finding it now through this new femininist movement which is linked up with the cause of Women's Suffrage. The Eighth Year produces many suffragettes, militant and otherwise. At first, in the first years of their married life, they scoffed at the idea of Votes for Women. They could not see the sense of it. They hated the vulgarities of the business, the shamelessness of it, the ugly squalor of these scuffles with the police, these fights with the crowds, these raids on the House of Commons. It was opposed to all their ideals of femininity and to all their traditions of girlhood. "The hussies ought to be whipped," is the verdict of the young wife in the first stage of her romantic affection. But, later on, when romance has worn very threadbare in the little home, when reality is beginning to poke its head through the drawing-room windows, she finds herself taking an interest in this strange manifestation which seems to be inspired by some kind of madness. She is silent now when some new phase in the conflict is being discussed in her presence. She listens and ponders. Presently she goes out of her way to get introduced to some suffrage woman on the outskirts of her acquaintance. She is surprised to find her a wonderfully cheerful, and apparently sane, woman, very keen, very alert, and with a great sense of humor—utterly unlike her tired, bored and melancholy self. Perhaps she is quite a young woman, a bachelor girl, earning her own living, down in Chelsea, or as a typist secretary in the City. But young as she is she has dived into all sorts of queer studies—the relations between men and women, the divorce laws, the science of eugenics—and she discusses them with an amazing frankness, and in a most revolutionary spirit, startling, and a little appalling, at first to this wife in her Eighth Year. She has made up her mind conclusively on all the great questions of life. She pooh-poohs romantic love. "There is too much fuss made about it," she says. "It is a mere episode, like influenza. There are bigger things." She holds herself perfectly free to choose her mate, and to remedy any little mistake which she may make in her choice. At present she prefers her independence and her own job, which she likes, thank you very much. She is tremendously enthusiastic about the work which women have got to do in the world, and there is nothing they cannot do, in her opinion. She claims an absolute equality with men. In fact, she is inclined to claim a superiority. After all, men are poor things.... Altogether she is a most remarkable young woman, and she seems to get tremendous fun out of life—and this wife in her Eighth Year, without agreeing with her yet envies her!

Or perhaps the wife meets a suffrage woman of middle-age. She, too, is a cheerful, keen, alert, bustling woman with cut-and-dried opinions on subjects about which the wife in the Eighth Year is full of doubt and perplexity. She has a certain hardness of character. She is intellectually hard, and without an atom of old-fashioned sentiment. She calls a spade a spade, in a rather embarrassing way, and prefers her facts to be naked. She is the mother of two children, whom she is bringing up on strictly eugenic principles, whatever those may be, and she is the wife of a husband whom she keeps in the background and treats as a negligible quantity. "We wives, my dear," she says, "have been too long kept prisoners in upholstered cages. It is time we broke our prison windows. I am breaking other people's windows as well. It lets in a lot of fresh air."

She talks a great deal about sweated labor, about the white-slave traffic, about women's work and wages. She talks still more about the treachery of the Government, the lies of politicians, the cowardice of men. "Oh, we are going to make them sit up. We shall stop at nothing. It is a revolution."

She is amazed at the ignorance of the young wife. "Good heavens, your education *has* been neglected!" she cries. "You are like all these stuffy suburban women, who are as ignorant of life as bunny-rabbits. Haven't you even read John Stuart Mill's *Subjection of Women?* Good gracious! Well, I will send you round some literature. It will open your eyes, my dear."

She sends round a lot of little pamphlets, full of dangerous ideas, ideas that sting like bees, ideas that are rather frightening to the wife in her Eighth Year. They refer to other books, which she gets out of the lending library. She reads Ibsen, and recognizes herself in many of those forlorn women in the plays. She reads small booklets on the Rights of Wives, on the Problems of Motherhood, on the Justice of the Vote. And suddenly, after a period of intellectual apathy, she is set on fire by all these burning sparks. She is caught up in a great flame of enthusiasm. It is like strong drink to her. It is like religious mania. She wakens out of her lethargy. Her feeling of boredom vanishes, gives way to a great excitement, a great exhilaration. She startles her husband, who thinks she has gone mad. She argues with him, laughs at his old-fashioned opinions, scoffs at him, pities him for his blindness. She goes out to suffrage meetings, starts to her feet one day and falters out a few excited words. She sits down with burning cheeks, with the sound of applause in her ears, like the roar of the sea. She learns to speak, to express herself coherently. She offers herself to "the cause." She sells her trinkets and gives the money to the funds. She is out for any kind of adventure, however perilous. She is one of the Hot Young Bloods, or if she has not the pluck for that, or the strength, one of the intellectual firebrands who are really more dangerous.

It is a queer business, this suffrage movement, which sets these women aflame. There are a few women in it who have the cold intellectual logic of John Stuart Mill himself. They have thought the thing out on scientific lines, in its economic, political, and social aspects. They want the vote honestly, as a weapon to give their sex greater power, greater independence, better conditions of life in the labor market. But the rank and file have no such intellectual purpose, though they make use of the same arguments and believe that these are the mainsprings of their actions. In reality they are Eighth Year women. That is to say, they seize upon the movement with a feverish desire to find in it some new motive in life, some tremendous excitement, some ideals greater and more thrilling than the little ideals of their home life. In this movement, in this great battle, they see many things which they keep secret. They go into it with blind impulses, which they do not understand, except vaguely. It is a movement of revolt against all the trammels of sex relationship which have come down through savagery to civilization; laws evolved out of the inherited experience of tribes and races for the protection of womanhood and the functions of womanhood, laws of repression, of restraint, for the sake of the children of the race; duties exacted by the social code again for the sake of the next generation. Having revolted against the duties of motherhood, all these laws, these trammels, these fetters, become to them intolerable, meaningless, exasperating. The scheme of monogamy breaks down. It has no deep moral purpose behind it, because the family is not complete. The scheme has been frustrated by the childlessness of the wife. Again, this movement is a revolt against the whole structure of modern society as it affects the woman—against the very architecture of the home; against all those tiny flats, those small suburban houses, in which women are cramped and confined, and cut off from the large world. It did not matter so long as there was a large world within the four walls. Their space was big enough to hold the big ideals of old-fashioned womanhood, in which the upbringing of children was foremost and all-absorbing. But for a woman who has lost these ideals and the duties that result from them, these little places are too narrow for their restless hearts; they become like prison cells, in which their spirits go pacing up and down, up and down, to come up against the walls, to heat their hands against them. They believe that they may find in this suffrage movement the key to the riddle of the mysteries in their souls, world-old mysteries, of yearnings for the Unknown Good, of cravings for the Eternal Satisfaction, for the perfect fulfilment of their beings. Their poor husband, a dear good fellow, after all, now that they look at him without hysteria, has not provided this Eternal Satisfaction. He has only provided pretty frocks, tickets for matinées, foolish little luxuries. He does not stand for them as the Unknown Good. After the first year or two of marriage they know him with all his faults and flaws, and familiarity breeds contempt. But here, in this struggle for the Vote, in these window-breakings and house-burnings, in imprisonments and forcible feedings, in this solidarity of women inspired by a fierce fanaticism—there is, they think, the answer to all their unsolved questions, the splendor and the glory of their sex, the possibility of magnificent promises and gifts, in which the soul of woman may at last find peace, and her body its liberty. She is to have the supreme mastery over her own spirit and flesh.

It is a fine promise. But as yet it is unfulfilled. It is not to be denied that for a time at least some of these women do gain a cheerfulness, a keenness, a vitality, which seem to be a great recompense for their struggles and strivings. But they are the younger women, and especially the young unmarried women, who get a good deal of fun out of all this excitement, all this adventure, all the dangerous defiance of law and convention. The older women—many of them—are already suffering a sad disillusionment. They have not yet found those splendid things which seemed at last within their grasp. They are desperate to get them, fierce in their desire for them, but the cup of wine is withheld from their lips. They find themselves growing old and still unsatisfied, growing hard, and' bitter, and revengeful against those who thwart them. The problems of their sex still remain with them. They may break all the laws, but get no nearer to liberty. They are still prisoners of fate, bond-slaves to a nature which they do not understand. The femininist movement is only a temporary way of escape for the wife who has reached her crisis in the Eighth Year.

CHAPTER IX

There is another way, and it has many doors. It is religion. Many of these women "take to religion" as they take to the suffrage movement, and find the same emotional excitement and adventure in it. They are caught up in it as by a burning flame. It satisfies something of their yearnings and desires. And it is a curious and lamentable thing that although it has been proved conclusively by all masters of philosophy and by all great thinkers, that some form of religion, is an essential need in the heart of women, the whole tendency of the time is to rob them of this spiritual guidance and comfort. Religion is not a part of the social scheme of things in "intellectual mansions" and in the small suburban houses of the professional classes. It is not entirely wiped off the slate, but it is regarded with indifference and as of no vital account in the sum of daily life. Occasionally a certain homage is paid to it, as to a pleasant, old-fashioned ritual which belongs to the code of "good form." In their courting days the young man and woman went to church now and then on a Sunday morning or a Sunday evening and held the same hymn-book, and enjoyed a little spiritual sentiment. They were married in church to the music of the Wedding March played by the organist. Sometimes as the years pass they drop into a service where there is good singing, a popular preacher, and a fashionable congregation. They regard themselves as Christians, and condescend to acknowledge the existence of God, in a vague, tolerant kind of way. But they do not enter into any intimate relations with God. He is not down on their visiting list. Many of them do not even go as far as those people I have described who regard God as part of the social code of "good form." They become frankly agnostic and smile at their neighbors who put on top-hats and silk dresses and stroll to church on a Sunday morning. It seems to them absurdly "Early Victorian." For they have read a great number of little books by the latest writers, who publish their philosophy in sevenpenny editions, and they have reached an intellectual position when they have a smattering of knowledge on the subject of evolution, anthropology, the origins of religion, literature and dogma, and the higher criticism. They have also read extracts from the works of Nietzsche, Kant, and the great free-thinkers, or reviews of their works in the halfpenny newspapers. The ideas of the great thinkers and great rebels have filtered down to them through the writings of little thinkers and little rebels. They have been amused by the audacities of Bernard Shaw and other intellectuals of their own age. They have read the novels of H. G. Wells, which seem to put God in His right place. They have imbibed unconsciously the atmosphere of free-thought and religious indifference which comes through the open windows, through the keyholes, through every nook and cranny. Occasionally the husband lays down the law on the subject with dogmatic agnosticism, or dismisses the whole business of religion with a laugh as a matter of no importance either way, certainly as a problem not worth bothering about.

So the wife's spiritual nature is starved. She is not even conscious of it, except just now and then when she is aware of a kind of spiritual hunger, or when she has little thoughts of terror at the idea of death, or when she is in low spirits. She has no firm and certain faith to which she can cling in moments of perplexity. She has no belief in any divine authority from which she can seek guidance for her actions. There is no supernatural influence about her from which she can draw any sweetness of consolation, when the drudgery and monotony of life begins to pall on her. When temptations come she has no anchor holding her fast to duty and honor. She has no tremendous ideals giving a large meaning to the little things of life. She has no spiritual vision to explain the mysteries of her own heart, or any spiritual balm to ease its pain and restlessness. She must rely always on her common sense, on her own experience, on her own poor little principles of what is right or wrong, or expedient, or "the proper thing." When those fail her, all fails; she is helpless, like a ship without a rudder, like a straw in the eddy of a mill race.

It is just at this time, when all has failed her, and when she seems to be drifting helplessly, that she is ready for religion, a bundle of dry straw which will burst into flame at the touch of a spark, a spiritual appetite hungry for food. In hundreds of cases these women take to the queerest kinds of spiritual food, some of it very poisonous stuff. Any impostor with a new creed may get hold of them. Any false prophet may dupe them into allegiance. They get into the hands of peculiar people. They are tempted to go to a spiritualistic séance and listen to the jargon of spiritualism. It frightens them at first, but after their first fears, and a little shrinking horror, they go forward into these "mysteries," and are obsessed by them. It appears they are "psychical." Undoubtedly after a little practice they could get into touch with the spirit-world. With planchette and table-rapping, and with mediumistic guidance, they may learn the secrets of the ghost-world, and invoke the aid of spirits in their little household. It becomes a mania with them. It becomes, in many cases, sheer madness.

There are other women who seek their spiritual salvation among the clairvoyants and crystal-gazers and palmists of the West End.

They become devotees of the Black Art, and dupes of those who prey upon the Eternal Gullible. There are others who join the Christian Scientists, and find the key to the riddle of life in the writings of Mrs. Eddy. They experiment in will-power—upon their unfortunate husbands. They adopt the simple life, and bring themselves into a low state of health by fruit diet. They learn a new language full of strange technical terms, which they but dimly understand, yet find comforting, like the old woman and her Mesopotamia, which was a blessèd word to her. But in spite of all its falsity and folly, it does give them a new interest in life, and lift them right out of the ruck of suburban dulness. So far at least it is helpful to them. It is some kind of spiritual satisfaction, though afterwards, perhaps, they may fall into a spiritual excitement and hysteria worse than their old restlessness, and become a nuisance to their family and friends, women with *idées fixes*.

It is better for them if they can grope their way back to the old Christian faith, with its sweetness and serenity and divine ideals. Here at last the woman may find authority, not to be argued about, not to be dodged, but to be obeyed. Here at last she may find tremendous ideals giving a significance to the little things of life, which seemed so trivial, so futile, and so purposeless. Here is wholesome food for her spiritual hunger, giving her new strength and courage, patience and resignation. Here are great moral lessons from which she may draw wisdom and guidance for her own poor perplexities. Then when temptations come, she may cling to an anchor of faith which will not slip in shifting sands, but is chained to a great rock. The wisdom of the Church, the accumulated experience stored up in the Church, the sweetness of all great Christian lives, the splendid serenity of the Christian laws, so stern and yet so tolerant, so hard and yet so easy, give to this woman's soul the peace she has desired, not to be found among the ghosts of modern spiritualism, nor in the pseudo-scientific jargon of Mrs. Eddy's works, nor in the glass-crystals of the clairvoyants. For the Christian faith has no use for hysteria; it exacts a healthy discipline of mind. It demands obedience to the laws of life, by which no woman may shirk the duties of her nature, or pander to her selfishness, or dodge the responsibilities of her state as a wife, or forget her marriage-vows and all that they involve.

There would be no fatal significance about the Eighth Year if the old religion were still of vital influence in the home. For after all, in spite of all our cleverness, we have not yet discovered any new intellectual formula or philosophy which will force men and women to do those things which are unpleasant but necessary to insure the future of the race; to deny themselves so that the future generation may gain; to suffer willingly in this world for the sake of an advantage in a future life. If people do not believe in a future life, and in such rewards as are offered by the Christian dogma, they prefer to have their advantages here and now. But as we know, if we face the facts of life clearly, the advantages, here and now, are not easy to get. Life, at its best, is a disappointing business. There is a lot of rough with the smooth, especially for women, especially for those women of the middle-classes in small suburban homes, over-intel-lectualized, with highly strung nerves, in a narrow environment, without many interests, and without much work. It is just because many of them are entirely without religion to give some great purpose to their inevitable trivialities that their moral perspective becomes hopelessly inverted, as though they were gazing through the wrong end of the telescope. Having no banking account in the next life, they spend themselves in this life, and live "on tick," as it were. Religion is the gospel of unselfishness. Lacking religion, they are utterly selfish. They do not worry about the future of the race. Why should they? All they are worrying about is to save themselves pain, expense, drudgery. Children are a great nuisance—therefore they will not have children. They want to put in a good time, to enjoy youth and beauty as long as possible, to get as much fun as they can here and now. But, as we have seen, the fun begins to peter out somewhere about the Eighth Year, and "the good time" has disappeared like a mirage when one gets close to it, and even youth and beauty are drooping and faded like yesterday's flowers.

What is the woman to do then? She is the victim of shattered illusions, of broken hopes. Before her is nothing but a gray vista of years. She has nothing to reconcile her with the boredom of her days, nothing to compensate her for domestic drudgery, no cure for the restlessness and feverishness which consume her, no laws by which she may keep straight. She sees crookedly, her spirit rushes about hither and thither. She is like a hunted thing, hunted by her desires, and she can find no sanctuary; no sanctuary unless she finds religion, and the right religion. There are not many women nowadays who find this way of escape, for religion has gone out of fashion, like last year's hats, and it wants a lot of pluck to wear a last year's hat.

CHAPTER X

Besides, the husband does not like it. He discourages religion, except in homoeopathic doses, taken by way of a little tonic, as one goes to the theatre for a pick-me-up. As he remarks, he does not believe in women being too spiritual. It is not "healthy." If his wife goes to church with any regularity he suspects there is an attractive cleric round the corner. And sometimes he is right. Anyhow, he does not feel the need of religion, except when he gets a pretty bad dose of influenza and has an uneasy thought that he is going to "peg out." As a rule he enjoys good health, and has no time to bother about the supernatural. He does not meet it in the city. It is not a marketable commodity. It is not, as he says, "in his line of country." He does not see why it should be in his wife's line of country. He is annoyed when his wife takes up any of these cranky ideas. He rages inwardly when she takes them up passionately. Why can't she be normal?

Why on earth can't she go on as she began, with her little feminine interests, keeping herself pretty for his sake, keen on the latest fashions, neighborly with young wives like herself, and fond of a bit of frivolity now and then? When she complains that she has idle hands in her lap, and wants something to do, he reminds her that she found plenty to do in the first years of her married life. When she cries out that she is bored, he points out to her that she gets much more amusement than he does.

And that is true, because by the time he has reached the Eighth Year he is pretty busy. Ambition has caught hold of him and he is making a career. It is not easy. Competition is deadly. He has got his work cut out to keep abreast with his competitors. It is a constant struggle "to keep his end up." He finds it disconcerting when he comes home in the evenings after the anxiety of his days, dog-tired and needing sympathy, to find that his wife has an attack of nerves, or a feverish desire to go out and "see something." He wants to stay at home and rest, to dawdle over the evening paper, to listen to a tune or two from his wife.

He would like her to bring his slippers to him, as she used to do in the old days, to hover round him a little with endearing words, and then, with not too much of *that*, to keep quiet, assenting to his opinions when he expresses them, and being restful. He has his own grievances. He is not without troubles of soul and body. He has had to face disappointment, disillusionment, hours of blank pessimism. He has had to get to grips with reality, after the romanticism of his youth, and to put a check upon his natural instincts and desires. In many ways it is harder for the man than for the woman. Civilization and the monogamous code have not been framed on easy lines for men. To keep the ordinary rules of his caste he must put a continual restraint upon himself, make many sacrifices. Women and wives forget that human nature has not changed because men wear black coats and tall hats instead of the skins of beasts. Human nature is exactly the same as it ever was, strong and savage, but it has to be tamed and repressed within the four walls of a flat in West Kensington, or within a semi-detached house at Wimbledon.

There are moments when the man hears the call of the wild, and loathes respectability and conventionality with a deadly loathing. In his heart, as in the heart of every man, there is a little Bohemia, a little country of lawlessness and errant fancy and primitive desires. Sometimes when he has shut himself up in his study, when the servants are in the kitchen washing up the supper-things, when his wife is lying down with a bad headache, he unlocks the door of that Bohemia in his heart, and his imagination goes roving, and he hears the pan-pipes calling, and the stamp of the cloven hoofs of the old Nature-god. He would like to cut and run sometimes from this respectable life of his, to go in search of adventure down forbidden pathways, and to find the joy of life again in Liberty Hall. This fretful wife of his, this social-ladder climbing, the whole business of "playing the game" in the same old way, makes him very tired, and gets on his nerves at times most damnably. He has his temptations. He hears siren voices calling him. He sees the lure of the witch-women. To feel his pulse thrill to the wine of life, to get the fever of joy in his blood again, to plunge into the fiery lake of passion, are temptations from which he does not escape because he is Something in the City, or a barrister-at-law, and a married man with a delicate wife. But, being a man, with a man's work, and a man's ambition, he keeps his sanity, and quite often his self-respect. His eyes are clear enough to see the notice-boards on the boundary lines of the forbidden territory, "Trespassers will be prosecuted," "Please keep off the grass," "No thoroughfare." He locks up the gate to the little Bohemia in his heart, and puts the key into a secret cupboard of his brain. He understands quite clearly that if he once "goes off the rails," as he calls it, his ambitions will be frustrated and his career spoiled. Besides, being a conventionalist and somewhat of a snob, he would hate to be found out in any violation of the social code, and his blood runs cold at the idea of his making a fool of himself with a woman, or anything of that kind. The creed of his social code, of the pot-hatted civilization, of this suburban conventionality of these little private snob-doms, is stronger in the man than in the woman. When she once takes the bit between her teeth, as it were, she becomes utterly lawless. But the man reins himself in more easily. He finds it on the whole less difficult to be law-abiding. He has also a clearer vision of the logic of things. He knows that certain results follow certain causes. He can measure up the consequences of an act, and weigh them. He is guided by his brain rather than by his emotions. He has certain fixed principles deeply rooted in him. He has a more delicate sense of honor than most women. It is summed up in that old school-phrase of his—"playing the game." However much his nerves may be jangled, and goodness knows they are often jangled, especially as the Eighth Year draws near, he is generally master of himself. At least he does not, as a rule, have hysterical outbursts, or give rein to passionate impulses, or suddenly take some wild plunge, upsetting all the balance of his life. He does not take frightful risks, as a woman will always take them, recklessly, when she reaches her crisis.

So it is that he looks coldly upon his wife's desires for some new emotional activity, of whatever kind it may be, religious, political, or ethical. He hates any symptoms of fanaticism. He shivers at any breach of good form. He would like her always to be sitting in the drawing-room when he comes home, in a pretty frock, with a novel in her lap, with a smile in her eyes. He does not and will not understand that this childless wife of his must have strong interests outside her little home to save her from eating her heart out. He hides from himself the fact that her childlessness is a curse which is blighting her. He pooh-poohs her tragic cry for help. He is just a little brutal with her when she accuses him of thwarting all the desires of her soul. And he is scared, thoroughly scared, when at last she takes flight, on wild wings, to some spiritual country, or to some moral, or immoral, territory, where he could not follow. He tries to call her back. But sometimes she may not be called back. She has escaped beyond the reach of his voice.

CHAPTER XI

Snobbishness is one of the causes which lead to the Eighth Year, and not the least among them. It is an essentially middle-class snobbishness, and has grown up, like a fungus growth, with that immense and increasing class of small, fairly well-to-do households who have come into being with the advance of material prosperity during the past twenty-five years, and with the progress of elementary education, and all that it has brought with it in the form of new desires for pleasure, amusement and more luxuries. These young husbands and wives who set up their little homes are not, as I have said, content to start on the same level as their parents in the first years of their married life. They must start at least on the level of their parents at the end of their married life, even a little in advance. The seeds of snobbishness are sown before marriage. The modern son pooh-poohs the habits of his old-fashioned father. They are not good enough for him. He has at least twice the pocket-money at school compared with the allowance of his father when he was a boy. He goes to a more expensive school and learns expensive habits. When he begins work he does not hand over most of his salary as his father used to hand over his salary a generation ago, to keep the family pot boiling. He keeps all that he earns, though he is still living at home, and develops a nice taste in clothes. One tie on week-days and another tie for Sundays are still good enough for the father, but the son buys ties by the dozen, and then has a passion for fancy socks, and lets his imagination rove into all departments of haberdashery. He is only a middle-class young man, but he dresses in the style of a man of fashion, adopts some of the pleasures of the man about town, and is rather scornful of the little house in the suburbs to which he returns after a bachelor's dinner in a smart restaurant, or after a tea-party with gaiety girls. He becomes a "Nut," and his evenings are devoted to a variety of amusements, which does away with a good deal of money. He smokes a special brand of cigarettes. He hires a motor-car occasionally for a spin down to Brighton. His mother and father are rather scared by this son who lives in a style utterly beyond their means.

The girl is a feminine type of the new style. She has adopted the new notions. At a very early age she is expert in all the arts of the younger generation, and at seventeen or eighteen has already revolted from the authority of her parents. She is quite a nice girl, naturally, but her chief vice is vanity. She is eaten up with it. It is a consuming passion. From the moment she gets out of bed in the morning for the first glimpse of her face in the looking-glass to the time she goes to bed after putting on some lip-salve and face enamel, she is absorbed with self-consciousness about her "looks." Her face is always occupying her attention. Even in railway trains she keeps biting her lips to make them red. At every window she passes she gives a sidelong glance to see if her face is getting on all right. Her main ambition in life is to be in the fashion. She is greedy for "pretty things" and sponges upon her father and mother for the wherewithal to buy them, and she will not lay a little finger on any work in the kitchen or even make a bed, lest her hands should be roughened and because it would not be quite "lady-like."

A pretty education for matrimony! A nice couple to set up house together Poor children of life, they are doomed to have a pack of troubles. Because as they began they go on, with the same ideas, with the same habits of mind, until they get a rude shock. Their little household is a shrine to the great god Snob. They are his worshippers. To make a show beyond their meansj or up to the very limit of their means, to pretend to be better off than they are, to hide any sign of poverty, to dress above their rank in life, to show themselves in places of entertainment, to shirk domestic drudgery, that is their creed.

In the old days, before the problem of the Eighth Year had arrived, the wives of men, the mothers of those very girls, kept themselves busy by hundreds of small duties. They made the beds, dusted the rooms, helped the servants in the kitchen, made a good many of their own clothes, mended them, altered them, cleaned the silver. But nowadays the wife of the professional man does none of these things if there is any escape from them. She keeps one servant at a time when her mother did without a servant. She keeps two servants as soon as her husband can afford an extra one, three servants if the house is large enough to hold them. Indeed, a rise in the social scale is immediately the excuse for an additional servant, and in the social status the exact financial prosperity of the middle-classes is reckoned by them according to the number of servants they keep. And whether it be two or three, the little snob wife sits in her drawing-room with idle hands, trying to kill time, getting tired of doing nothing, but proud of her laziness. And the snob husband encourages her in her laziness. He is proud of it, too. He would hate to think of his wife dusting, or cleaning, or washing up. He does not guess that this worship of his great god Snob is a devil's worship, having devilish results for himself and her. The idea that women want work never enters his head. His whole ambition in life is to prevent his wife from working, not only when he is alive, but after he is dead. He insures himself heavily and at the cost of a great financial strain upon his resources in order that "if anything happens" his wife, even then, need not raise her little finger to do any work. But something "happens" before he is dead. The woman revolts from the evil spell of her laziness. She finds some work for her idle hands to do—good work or bad.

CHAPTER XII

If only those idle women would find some good work to do the Eighth Year would lose its terrors. And there is so much good work to do if they would only lay their hands to it! If they cannot get in touch with God, they can at least get in touch with humanity. At their very doors there is a welter of suffering, struggling humanity craving for a little help, needing helping hands, on the very edge of the abyss of misery, and slipping down unless they get rescued in the nick of time. In the mean streets of life, in the hospitals, at the prison gates, in the reformatories, in the dark haunts of poverty, there are social workers striving and toiling and moiling in the service of all these seething masses of human beings. But there are too few of them, and the appeals for volunteers in the ranks of the unpaid helpers are not often answered. They are hardly ever answered from the class of women who have least in the world to do, and most need of such kinds of work. Many of these women have good voices. They sing little drawing-room ballads quite well, until they get sick of the sound of their own singing in their lonely little drawing-rooms. But they do not think of singing in the hospitals, and the workhouse wards, where their voices would give joy to suffering people, or miserable people who do not often hear the music of life. These women have no children. They have shirked the pains of childbirth. But they might help to give a little comfort and happiness to other mothers' children, to shepherd a small flock for a day's outing in the country, to organize the children's playtime, to nurse the sick baby now and then. These idle women remember their own girlhood and its dreams. They remember their own innocence, the shelter of their home-life. It would be good for them if they gave a little loving service to the girls in the working-quarters of the great cities, and went down into the girl-clubs to play their dance tunes, to keep them out of the streets, to give them a little innocent fun in the evenings. These lazy women cry out that they are prisoners in upholstered cages. But there are many prisoners in stone cells, who at the prison gates, on their release, stand looking out into the cold gray world, with blank, despairing eyes, with no prospect but that of crime and vice, unless some unknown friend comes with a little warmth of human love, with a quick sympathy and a ready helpfulness. Here is work for workless women who are well-to-do. They are unhappy in their own homes, because they are tired of its trivialities, tired of its little luxuries, bored to death with themselves because they have no purpose in life. But in the mean streets round the corner they would find women still clinging with extraordinary courage to homes that have no stick of furniture in them, amazingly cheerful, although instead of little luxuries they have not even the barest necessities of life, unwearied, indefatigable, heroic in endurance, though they toil on sweated wages. The women of the well-to-do middle-classes drift apart from their husbands because perhaps they have irritable little habits, because they do not understand all the yearnings in their wives' hearts, because they have fallen below the old ideals of their courting days. But here in the slums these women with a grievance would find other women loyal to their husbands who come home drunk at nights, loyal through thick and thin to husbands who "bash" them when they speak a sharp word, loyal to the death to husbands who are untamed brutes with only the love of the brute for its mate. There is no problem of the Eighth Year in Poverty Court, only the great problems of life and death, of hunger and thirst and cold, of labor and want of work. Here in the mean streets of the world is the great lesson that want of work is the greatest disaster, the greatest moral tragedy, that may happen to men and women.

If the idle women of the little snobdoms would come forth from their houses and flats, they would see that lesson staring them in the face, with a great warning to themselves. And if they would thrust aside their selfishness and learn the love of humanity, it would light a flame in their hearts which would kindle the dead ashes of their disillusionment and burn up their grievances, and make a bonfire of all their petty little troubles, and make such a light in their lives as would enable them to see the heroic qualities of ordinary duties bravely done, and of ordinary lives bravely led. Here they would find another way of escape from the perils of the Eighth Year, and a new moral health for their hearts and brains.

It is only now and then that some woman is lucky enough to find this way out, for snobbishness enchains them, and it is difficult to break its fetters.

CHAPTER XIII

When the woman has once taken flight, or is hesitating before taking her flight, in the Eighth Year, it is an almost hopeless business for the husband to call her back. Whenever she is called back, it is by some outside influence, beyond *his* sphere of influence, by some sudden accident, by some catastrophe involving both of them, or by some severe moral shock, shaking the foundations of their little home like an earthquake. There are cases in which the woman has been called back by the sudden smash-up of her husband's business, by financial ruin. In his social ladder-climbing he is too rash. One of the rungs of the ladder breaks beneath his feet and he comes toppling down. Owing to this deadly competition of modern life, he loses his "job." It is given to a younger or better man, or to a man with a stronger social pull. He comes home one day with a white face, trembling, horribly scared, afraid to break the news to a woman who has not been helpful to him of late, and of whose sympathy he is no longer sure. He believes that this misfortune is the last straw which will break their strained relations. He sees the great tragedy looming ahead, hearing down upon him. But, curiously enough, this apparent disaster is the salvation of both of them. The despair of her husband calls to the woman's loyalty. All her grievances against this man are suddenly swallowed up in the precipice which has opened beneath his feet. All her antagonism is broken down and dissolved into pity. Her self-pride is slain by this man's abasement. His weakness, his need of help, his panic-stricken heart cry to her. After all their drifting apart, their indifference to each other, their independence, he wants her again. He wants her as a helpmeet. He wants any courage she can give him, any wisdom. And she is glad to be wanted. She stretches out her hands to him. They clasp each other, and there is no longer a gulf beneath their feet; misfortune has built a bridge across the gulf which divided them. More than that, all the little meannesses of their life, all the petty selfishness of their days, all the little futile things over which they have wrangled and jangled are thrust on one side, and are seen in their right perspective. The things that matter, the only things that matter, are seen, perhaps, for the first time, clearly, in a bright light, now that they are face to face with stem realities. The shock throws them off their pedestals of conceit, of self-consciousness, of pretence. They stand on solid ground. The shock has broken the masks behind which they hid themselves. It has broken the hard crust about their hearts. It has shattered the idol which they worshipped, the idol of the great god Snob.

And so they stare into each other's soul, and take hands again like little children, abandoned by the Wicked Uncles of life, and they grope their way back to primitive things, and begin the journey again. They have found out that this new comradeship is better even than the old romantic love of their courting days. They have discovered something of the great secret of life. They are humbled. They make new pledges to each other, pick up the broken pieces of their hopes and dreams and fit them together again in a new and sounder scheme. This time, in some cases, they do not leave the baby out of the business. The wife becomes a mother, and the child chases away all the ghosts which haunted her in the Eighth Year. She no longer wants to take flight. She has been called back.

It is nearly always some accident like this which calls the wife back, some sudden, startling change in the situation, caused by outside influences, or by the hand of Fate. Sometimes it is an illness which overtakes the husband or wife. Holding hands by the bedside, they stare into the face of Death, and again the trivialities of life, the pettiness of their previous desires, the folly of their selfishness, the stupidity of their little snobdom, are revealed by the whisperings of Death, and by its warnings. The truth of things stalks into the bedroom where the husband, or the wife, lies sleeping on the borderland. About the sick bed the weeping woman makes new vows, tears wash out her vanity, her self-conceit. Or, kneeling by the side of the woman whose transparent hand he clasps above the coverlet, the husband listens to the little voice within his conscience, and understands, with a great heartache, the pitiful meaning of the domestic strife which seemed to have killed his love for the woman for whose life now he makes a passionate cry. In the period of convalescence, after Death has stolen away, when life smiles again through the open windows, that man and woman get back to sanity and to wisdom beyond that of common-sense. They begin again with new ideals. Perhaps in a little while one of the rooms becomes a nursery.

They get back to the joy of youth, once more the woman has been called back.

If none of these "accidents" happen, if some great influence like this does not thrust its way into the lives of this husband and wife during the crisis of the Eighth Year, if the woman is not caught up by some great enthusiasm, or if she can find no work for the idle hands to do, giving her new and absorbing interests to satisfy her heart and brain, then the Eighth Year is a fatal year, and the President of the Divorce Court has a new case added to his list, or the family records of the country chronicle another separation, or another woman goes to prison for arson or bomb-throwing. Because the laws of psychology are not so erratic as the world imagines. They work out on definite lines. Certain psychological forces having been set in motion, they lead inevitably to certain results. When once a woman has lost her interest in her home and husband, when she has become bored with herself, when she has a morbid craving for excitement and adventures, when she has become peevish and listless and hungry-hearted, she cannot remain in this condition. Those forces within her are tremendously powerful. They must find some outlet. They must reach a definite time of crisis when things have got to happen. These vague yearnings must be satisfied, somehow, anyhow. The emptiness of her heart must be filled by something or other. She will search round with wondering, wistful eyes, more desperate day by day, until she finds the thing, however evil it may be, however dangerous. She must still that throbbing brain of hers, even if she has to take drugs to do so. In spite of all the poison laws, she will find some kind of poison, some subtle and insidious drug to give her temporary cure, a period of vitality, a thrill of excitement, a glittering dream or two, a relief from the dulness which is pressing down upon her with leaden weights. She knows the penalty which follows this drug-taking—the awful reaction, the deadly lethargy that follows, the nervous crises, the loss of will-power, but she is prepared to pay the price because for a little while she gets peace, and artificial life. The family doctors know the prevalence of those drug-taking habits. They know the cause of them, they have watched the pitiful drama of these women's lives. But they can do nothing to cut out the cause. Not even the surgeon's knife can do that; their warnings fall on deaf ears, or are answered by a hysterical laugh.

As I have shown, there are other forms of drug-taking not less dangerous in their moral effects. If the woman does not go to the chemist's shop, she goes to the darkened room of the clairvoyant and the crystal-gazer, or to the spiritualistic séance, or to the man who hides his time until the crisis of the Eighth Year delivers the woman into his hands.

Here, then, frankly and in detail, I have set out the meaning of this dangerous year of married life, and have endeavored, honestly, to analyze all the social and psychological forces which go to make that crisis. It is, in some measure, a study of our modern conditions of life as they prevail among the middle-classes, so that the problem is not abnormal, but is present, to some extent, in hundreds of thousands of small households to-day. All the tendencies of the time, all the revolutionary ideas that are in the very air we breathe, all this modern spirit of revolt against disagreeable duties, and drudgery, and discipline, the decay of religious authority, the sapping of spiritual faith, the striving for social success, the cult of snobbishness, the new creed of selfishness which ignores the future of the race and demands a good time here and now, the lack of any ideals larger than private interests and personal comforts, the ignorance of men and women who call themselves intellectual, the nervous irritability of husbands and wives who live up to the last penny of their incomes, above all the childlessness of these women who live in small flats and suburban villas, and their utter laziness, all those signs and symptoms of our social sickness lead up, inevitably, and with fatal logic, to the tragedy of the Eighth Year.

PART II
A DEMONSTRATION

CHAPTER I

In the drawing-room of a flat in Intellectual Mansions, S. W., there was an air of quietude and peace. No one would have imagined for a moment that the atmosphere was charged with electricity, or that the scene was set for a drama of emotional interest with tragic potentialities. It seemed the dwelling-place of middle-class culture and well-to-do gentility.

The room was furnished in the "New Art" style, as seen in the showrooms of the great stores. There were sentimental pictures on the walls framed in dark oak. The sofa and chairs were covered in a rather flamboyant chintz. Through the French windows at the back could be seen the balcony railings, and, beyond, a bird's-eye view of the park. A piano-organ in the street below was playing the latest ragtime melody, and there was the noise of a great number of whistles calling for taxis, which did not seem to come.

In a stiff-backed arm-chair by the fireplace sat an elderly lady, of a somewhat austere appearance, who was examining through her spectacles the cover of a paper backed novel, depicting a voluptuous young woman; obviously displeasing to her sense of propriety. Mrs. Heywood's sense of propriety was somewhat acutely developed, to the annoyance, at times, of Mollie, the maid-servant, who was clearing away the tea-things in a bad temper. That is to say, she was making a great deal of unnecessary clatter.

Mrs. Heywood ignored the clatter, and concentrated her attention on the cover of the paper-backed book. It seemed to distress her, and presently she gave expression to her distress.

"Dear me! What an improper young woman!"

Mollie's bad temper was revealed by a sudden tightening of the lips and a flushed face. She bent across an "occasional" table and peered over the old lady's shoulder, and spoke rather impudently.

"Excuse me, ma'am, but that's *my* novel, if you don't mind."

"I *do* mind," said Mrs. Heywood. "I was shocked to find it on the kitchen dresser."

Molly tossed her head, so that her white cap assumed an acute angle.

"I was shocked to see that it had gone from the kitchen dresser."

Then she lowered her voice and added in a tone of bitter grievance—

"Blessed if one can call anything one's own in this here flat."

"It's not fit literature for *any* young girl," said Mrs. Heywood severely. She looked again at the flaunting lady with an air of extreme disapproval.

"Disgusting!"

Mollie rattled the tea-things violently.

"It's good enough for the mistress, anyhow."

Mrs. Heywood was surprised.

"Surely she did not lend it to you?"

"Well—not exactly," said Mollie, with just a trace of embarrassment. "I borrowed it. It's written by her particular friend, Mr. Bradshaw."

"Mr. Bradshaw! Surely not?"

The old lady wiped her spectacles rather nervously.

"A very nice-spoken gentleman," said Mollie, "though he does write novels."

Mrs. Heywood looked at the author's name for the first time and expressed her astonishment.

"Good gracious! So it is."

Mollie laughed as she folded up the tea-cloth. She had gained a little triumph, and scored off the "mother-in-law," as she called the elderly lady, in the kitchen.

"Oh, he knows a thing or two, he does, my word!"

She winked solemnly at herself in the mirror over the mantelshelf.

"Hold your tongue, Mollie," said Mrs. Heywood sharply.

"Servants are not supposed to have any tongues. Oh, dear no!"

With this sarcastic retort Mollie proceeded to put the sugar-basin into the china-cupboard, but seemed to expect a counter-attack. She was not disappointed.

"Mollie!" said Mrs. Heywood severely, looking over the rims of her spectacles.

"Now what's wrong?"

"You have not cleaned the silver lately."

"Haven't I?" said Mollie sweetly.

"No," said Mrs. Heywood. "Why not, I should like to know?"

Mollie's "sweetness" was suddenly embittered. She spoke with ferocity.

"If you want to know, it's because I won't obey two mistresses at once. There's no liberty for a mortal soul in this here flat. So there!"

"Very well, Mollie," said Mrs. Heywood mildly. "We will wait until your mistress comes home. If she has any strength of mind at all she will give you a month's notice."

Mollie sniffed. The idea seemed to amuse her.

"The poor dear hasn't any strength of mind."

"I am surprised at you, Mollie."

"That's why she has gone to church again."

Mrs. Heywood was startled. She was so startled that she forgot her anger with the maid.

"Again? Are you sure?"

"Well, she had a look of church in her eyes when she went out."

"What sort of a look?" asked Mrs. Heywood.

"A stained-glass-window look."

Mrs. Heywood spoke rather to herself than to Mollie.

"That makes the third time to-day," she said pensively.

Mollie spoke mysteriously. She too had forgotten her anger and impudence. She dropped her voice to a confidential tone.

"The mistress is in a bad way, to my thinking. I've seen it coming on."

"Seen what coming on?" asked the elderly lady.

"She sits brooding too much. Doesn't even pitch into me when I break things. That's a bad sign."

"A bad sign?"

"I've noticed they're all taken like this when they go wrong," said the girl, speaking as one who had had a long experience of human nature in Intellectual Mansions, S. W. But these words aroused the old lady's wrath.

"How dare you!" said Mrs. Heywood. "Leave the room at once."

"I must tell the truth if I died for it," said Mollie.

The two women were silent for a moment, for just then a voice outside called, "Clare! Clare!" rather impatiently.

"Oh, Lord!" said Mollie. "There's the master."

"Clare!" called the voice. "Oh, confound the thing!"

"I suppose he's lost his stud again," said Mollie. "He always does on club nights. I'd best be off."

She took up the tea-tray and left the room hurriedly, just as her master came in. It was Mr. Herbert Heywood, generally described by his neighbors as being "Something in the City"—a man of about thirty, slight, clean-shaven, boyish, good-looking, with nervous movements and extreme irritability. He was in evening clothes with his tie undone.

"Plague take this tie!" he growled, making use of one or two un-Parliamentary expressions. Then he saw his mother and apologized.

"Oh, I beg your pardon, mother. Where's Clare?"

Mrs. Heywood answered her son gloomily.

"I think she's gone to church again."

"Again?" said Herbert Heywood. "Why, dash it all—I beg your pardon, mother—she's always going to church now. What's the attraction?"

"I think she must be unwell," said Mrs. Hey-wood. "I've thought so for some time."

"Oh, nonsense! She's perfectly fit.... See if you can tie this bow, mother."

Mrs. Heywood endeavored to do so, and during the process her son showed great impatience and made irritable grimaces. But he returned to the subject of his wife.

"Perhaps her nerves are a bit wrong. Women are nervy creatures.... Oh, hang it all, mother, don't strangle me!... As I tell her, what's the good of having a park at your front door—Oh, thanks, that's better."

He looked at himself in the glass, and dabbed his face with a handkerchief.

"Of course I cut myself to-night. I always do when I go to the club."

"Herbert, dear," said Mrs. Heywood rather nervously.

"I—I suppose Clare is not going to bless you with a child?"

"*In this flat!*"

Herbert was startled and horrified. It was a great shock to him. He gazed round the little drawing-room rather wildly.

"Oh, Lord!" he said presently, when he had calmed down a little. "Don't suggest such a thing. Besides, she is not."

"Well, I'm nervous about her," said Mrs. Heywood.

"Oh, rats, mother! I mean, don't be so fanciful."

"I don't like this sudden craving for religion, Herbert. It's unhealthy."

"Devilish unhealthy," said Herbert.

He searched about vainly for his patent boots, which were in an obvious position. It added to his annoyance and irritability.

"Why can't she stay at home and look after me? I can't find a single damn thing. I beg your pardon, mother.... Women's place is in the home.... Now where on earth——"

He resumed his search for the very obvious patent boots and at last discovered them.

"Oh, there they are!"

He glanced at the clock, and expressed the opinion that he would be late for the club if he did not "look sharp." Then a little tragedy happened, and he gave a grunt of dismay when a bootlace broke.

"Oh, my hat! Why doesn't Clare look after my things properly?"

Mrs. Heywood asked another question, ignoring the broken bootlace.

"Need you go to the club to-night, Herbert?"

Herbert was both astonished and annoyed at this remark.

"Of course I must. It's Friday night and the one little bit of Bohemianism I get in the week. Why not?"

"Oh, I don't know," said Mrs. Heywood meekly. "Except that I thought Clare is feeling rather lonely."

"Lonely?" said Herbert. "She has you, hasn't she?"

"Yes, she has me."

Mrs. Heywood spoke as though that might be a doubtful consolation.

"Besides, what more does she want? She has her afternoon At Homes, hasn't she?"

"Yes, dear," said Mrs. Heywood, still more doubtfully.

"And she can always go to a matinée if she wants to, can't she?"

"Yes, dear."

"Then I have taken out a subscription to Mudie's for her, haven't I?"

Herbert Heywood spoke as though his wife had all the blessings of life, as though he had provided her with all that a woman's heart might desire. But Mrs. Heywood interrupted his catalogue of good things.

"I think she reads too many novels," she said.

"Oh, they broaden her mind," said Herbert. "Although, I must confess they bore *me* to death.... Now what have I done with my cigarette-case?"

He felt all over his pockets, but could not find the desired thing.

"Oh, the curse of pockets!"

"Some of them are very dangerous, Herbert."

"What, pockets?"

"No, novels," said Mrs. Heywood. "Look at this."

She thrust under his eyes the novel with the picture of the flaming lady.

"Gee whizz!" said Herbert, laughing. "Oh, well, she's a married woman."

"Do you see who the author is, Herbert?" Herbert look, and was astonished.

"Gerald Bradshaw, by Jove! Does he write this sort of muck?"

"He has been coming here rather often lately. Especially on club-nights, Herbert." Herbert Heywood showed distinct signs of annoyance.

"Does he, by Jove? I don't like the fellow. He's a particularly fine specimen of a bad hat."

"I'm afraid he's an immoral man," said Mrs. Heywood.

Herbert shrugged his shoulders.

"Well, Clare can take care of herself."

"I wonder," said Mrs. Heywood, as though she were not at all sure. "My dear, I think you ought to keep an eye on your wife just now."

Herbert Heywood took his eye-glass out of a fob pocket and fumbled with it.

"Keep an eye on her, mother?"

"She is very queer," said Mrs. Heywood. "I can't do anything to please her."

"Well, there's nothing strange in that," said Herbert. Then he added hastily—

"I mean it's no new symptom."

Mrs. Heywood stared at her son in a peculiar, significant way.

"She looks as if something is going to—happen."

Herbert was really startled.

"Happen? How? When?"

"I can't exactly explain. She appears to be waiting for something—or some one."

Herbert was completely mystified.

"I didn't keep her waiting this evening, did I?"

"I don't mean you, dear," said Mrs. Heywood.

"No?—Who, then?" asked Herbert.

Mrs. Heywood replied somewhat enigmatically. She gave a deep sigh and said—

"We women are queer things!"

"Queer isn't the word," said Herbert.

He stared at the carpet in a gloomy, thoughtful way, as though the pattern were perplexing him.

"Perhaps you're right about the novels. They've been giving her notions, or something."

Mrs. Heywood crossed the room hurriedly and went over to a drawer in a cabinet, from which she pulled out a number of pamphlets.

"Herbert," she said solemnly, "she doesn't read only novels. Look here. Look at all these little books. She simply devours them, Herbert, and then hides them."

"Naturally, after she has devoured them," said Herbert irritably. "But what the deuce are they?"

He turned them over one by one, reading out the titles, raising his eyebrows, and then whistling with surprise, and finally looking quite panic-stricken.

"*Women's Work and Wages*. Oh, Lord! John Stuart Mill on *The Subjection of Women*. *The Ethics of Ibsen*. Great Scott! *The Principles of Eugenics*.... My hat!"

"Quite so, Herbert," said Mrs. Heywood, with a kind of grim satisfaction in his consternation.

"I don't mind her reading improper novels," said Herbert, "but I draw the line at this sort of stuff."

"It's most dangerous."

"It's rank poison."

"That's what I think," said Mrs. Heywood.

"Where did she get hold of them?" asked Herbert.

Mrs. Heywood looked at her son as though she had another startling announcement.

"From that woman, Miss Vernon, the artist girl who lives in the flat above."

"What, that girl who throws orange-peel over the balcony?"

"Yes, the girl who is always whistling for taxis," said Mrs. Heywood.

"What, you mean the one who complained about my singing in the bath?"

"Yes, I shall never forgive her for that."

"Said she didn't mind if I sang in tune."

"Yes, the one who sells a Suffragette paper outside Victoria Station."

"It's the sort of thing she would do," said Herbert, with great sarcasm.

"I never liked her, my dear," said Mrs. Heywood.

"Confound her impudence! As if a British subject hasn't an inalienable right to sing in his bath! She had the cheek to say I was spoiling her temper for the rest of the day."

Mrs. Heywood laughed rather bitterly. "She looks as if she had a temper!"

Herbert gave the pamphlets an angry slap with the back of his hand and let them fall on the floor.

"Do you mean to say *she* has been giving Clare these pestilential things?"

"I saw her bring them here," said Mrs. Hey-wood.

"Well, they shan't stay here."

Herbert went to the fireplace and took up the tongs. Then he picked up the pamphlets as though they might bite and tossed them into the flames.

"Beastly things! Burn, won't you?"

He gave them a savage poke, deeper into the fire, and watched them smolder and then break into flame.

"Pestilential nonsense!... That's a good deed done, anyhow!"

Mrs. Heywood was rather scared.

"I am afraid Clare will be very angry."

"Angry! I shall give her a piece of my mind. She had no right to conceal these things." He spoke with dignity. "It isn't honorable."

"No," said Mrs. Heywood, "but all the same, dear, I wish you hadn't burned the books."

"I should like to burn the authors of 'em," said Herbert fiercely. "However, they'll roast sooner or later, that's a comfort."

"You had better be careful, dear," said Mrs. Heywood rather nervously. "Clare is in a rather dangerous frame of mind just now."

"Clare will have to learn obedience to her husband's wishes," said Herbert. "I thought she had learned by this time. She's been very quiet lately."

"Too quiet, Herbert. It's when we women are very quiet that we are most dangerous." Herbert was beginning to feel alarmed. He did not like all these hints, all these vague and mysterious suggestions.

"Good Lord, mother, you give me the creeps. Why don't you speak plainly?"

Mrs. Heywood was listening. She seemed to hear some sounds in the hall. Suddenly she retreated to her arm-chair and made a pretence of searching for her knitting.

"Hush!" she said. "Here she comes."

As she spoke the words, the door opened slowly and Clare came in. She was a tall, elegant woman of about thirty, with a quiet manner and melancholy eyes in which there was a great wistfulness. She spoke rather wearily—

"Not gone yet, Herbert? You'll be late for the club."

Herbert looked at his wife curiously, as though trying to discover some of those symptoms to which his mother had alluded.

"I'm afraid that's your fault," he said.

"My fault?"

"Surely you ought to stay at home sometimes and help me to get off decently," said Herbert in an aggrieved way. "You know perfectly well my tie always goes wrong."

Clare sighed; and then smiled rather miserably.

"Why can't men learn to do their own ties? We're living in the twentieth century, aren't we?"

She took off her hat, and sat down with it in her lap.

"Oh, how my head aches to-night."

"Where have you been?" asked Herbert

"Yes, dear, where *have* you been?" asked Mrs. Heywood.

"I've been round to church for a few minutes," said Clare.

"What on earth for?" asked Herbert impatiently.

"What does one go to church for?"

"God knows!" said Herbert bitterly.

"Precisely. Have you any objection?"

"Yes, I have."

Herbert spoke with some severity, as though he had many objections.

"I don't object to you going to your club," said Clare.

"Oh, that's different."

"In what way?" asked Clare.

"In every way. I am a man, and you're a woman."

Clare Heywood thought this answer out. She seemed to find something in the argument.

"Yes," she said, "it does make a lot of difference."

"I object strongly to this religious craze of yours," said Herbert, trying to be calm and reasonable. "It's unnatural. It's—it's devilish absurd."

"It may keep me from—from doing other things," said Clare.

She spoke as though the words had some tragic significance.

"Why can't you stay at home and read a decent novel?"

"It is so difficult to find a *decent* novel. And I am sick of them all."

"Well, play the piano, then," said Herbert.

"I am tired of playing the piano, especially when there is no one to listen."

"There's mother," said Herbert.

"Mother has no ear for music."

Mrs. Heywood was annoyed at this remark. It seemed to her unjust.

"How can you say so, Clare? You know I love Mozart."

"I haven't played Mozart for years," said Clare, laughing a little. "You are thinking of Mendelssohn."

"Well, it's all the same," said Mrs. Heywood.

"Yes, I suppose so," said Clare very wearily. She drooped her head and shut her eyes until suddenly she seemed to smell something.

"Is there anything burning?"

"Burning?" said Herbert nervously.

"There is a queer smell in the flat," said Clare.

Herbert stood with his back to the fire, and sniffed strenuously. "I can't smell anything."

"It's your fancy, dear," said Mrs. Heywood.

"It's the smell of burned paper," said Clare quite positively.

"Do you think so?" said her mother-in-law.

"Burned paper?" said Herbert.

Clare became suspicious. She leaned forward in her chair and stared into the fireplace.

"What are all those ashes in the grate?" she said.

"Oh, yes," said Herbert, as though he had suddenly remembered. "Of course I *have* been burning some papers."

"What papers?" asked Clare.

"Oh, old things," said Herbert rather hurriedly. "Well, I had better be off. Goodnight, mother."

He kissed her affectionately and said:

"Don't stay up late. I have taken the key, Clare."

"I hope it will fit the lock when you come back," said Clare.

She spoke the words very quietly, but for some reason they raised her husband's ire.

"For heaven's sake don't try to be funny, Clare."

"I wasn't trying," said Clare very calmly. For a moment Herbert hesitated. Then he came back to his wife and kissed her.

"I think we are both a bit irritable to-night, aren't we?"

"Are we?" said Clare.

"Nerves," said Herbert, "the curse of the age. Well, good-night."

Just as he was going out, Mollie, the maidservant, came in and said:

"It's Miss Vernon, ma'am."

"Oh," said Clare. She glanced at her husband for a moment and theft said:

"Well, bring her in, Mollie."

"Yes, ma'am," said Mollie, going out of the room again.

"Great Scott!" exclaimed Herbert, in a sudden excitement. "It's that woman who flings her beastly orange-peel into my window boxes. Clare, I strongly object——"

Clare answered him a little passionately: "Oh, I am tired of your objections."

"She's not a respectable character," said Herbert.

"Hush, Herbert!" said Mrs. Heywood.

As she spoke the girl who had been called Madge Vernon entered the room.

She was a bright, cheery girl, dressed plainly in a tailor-made coat and skirt, with brown boots.

"I thought I would look in for half-an-hour," she said very cheerfully to Clare. "If you are busy, send me packing, my dear."

"I am never busy," said Clare. "I have nothing in the world to do."

"Oh, that's rotten!" said Madge. "Can't you invent something? How are you, Mrs. Heywood?"

She shook hands with the old lady, who answered her greeting with a rather grim "Good evening."

"Herbert is going out to-night," said Clare. "By the way, you don't know my husband."

Madge Vernon looked at Herbert Heywood very sweetly.

"I have heard him singing. How do you do?"

Herbert was not at all pleased with her sweetness.

"Excuse me, won't you?" he said. "I am just off to my club."

"Don't you take your wife with you?" asked Miss Vernon.

"My wife! It's a man's club."

"Oh, I see. Men only. Rather selfish, isn't it?"

Herbert Heywood was frankly astonished.

"Selfish? Why selfish? Well, I won't stop to argue the point. Good-night, Clare. Doubtless you will enjoy Miss Vernon's remarkable and revolutionary ideas."

"I am sure I shall," said Clare.

Mrs. Heywood followed her son to the door.

"Be sure you put a muffler round your neck, dear."

Herbert answered his mother in a low voice, looking fiercely at Madge Vernon.

"I should like to twist it round somebody else's neck!"

"I will come and find it for you, dear."

The two young women were left alone together, and Clare brought forward a chair.

"Sit down, won't you? Here?"

A moment later the front door was heard to hang and at the sound of it Madge laughed a little.

"Funny things, husbands! I am sure I shouldn't know what to do with one."

Clare smiled wanly.

"One can't do anything with them."

"By the by," said Madge, "I have brought a new pamphlet for you. The 'Rights of Wives.'"

Clare took the small book nervously, as though it were a bomb which might go off at any moment.

"I have been reading those other pamphlets."

"Pretty good, eh?" said Madge, laughing. "Eye-openers! What?"

"They alarm me a little," said Clare. "Alarm you?" Madge Vernon was immensely amused. "Why, they don't bite!"

"Yes, they do," said Clare. "Here." She put her hand to her head as if it had been wounded.

"You mean they give you furiously to think? Well, that's good."

"I'm not sure," said Clare. "Since I began to think I have been very miserable."

"Oh, that will soon wear off," said Madge Vernon briskly. "You'll get used to it."

"It will always hurt," said Clare.

Madge Vernon smiled at her.

"I made a habit of it."

"It's best not to think," said Clare. "It's best to go on being stupid and self-satisfied."

Clare's visitor was shocked.

"Oh, not self-satisfied! That is intellectual death."

"There are other kinds of death," said Clare. "Moral death."

Madge Vernon raised her eyebrows.

"We must buck up and do things. That's the law of life."

"I have nothing to do," said Clare, in a pitiful way.

"How strange! I have such a million things to do. My days aren't long enough. I am always pottering about with one thing or another."

"What kind of things?" asked Clare wistfully.

Madge Vernon gave her a cheerful little laugh.

"For one thing, it's a great joke having to earn one's own living. The excitement of never knowing whether one can afford the next day's meal! The joy of painting pictures—which the Royal Academy will inevitably reject. The horrible delight of burning them when they are rejected.... Besides, I am a public character, I am."

"Are you? How?" asked Clare.

"A most notorious woman. I'm on the local Board of Guardians and all sorts of funny old committees for looking after everything and everybody."

"What do you do?"

Clare asked the question as though some deep mystery lay in the answer.

"Oh, I poke up the old stick-in-the-muds," said Madge Vernon, "and stir up no end of jolly rows. I make them do things, too; and they hate it. Oh, how they hate it!"

"What things, Madge?"

"Why, attending to drains, and starving widows, and dead dogs, and imbecile children, and people 'what won't work,' and people 'what will' but can't."

Clare laughed at this description and then became sad again.

"I envy you! I have nothing on earth to do, and my days are growing longer and longer, so that each one seems a year."

"Haven't you any housework to do?" asked Madge.

"Not since my husband could afford an extra servant."

Miss Vernon made an impatient little gesture.

"Oh, those extra servants! They have ruined hundreds of happy homes."

"Well, we have only got one now," said Clare. "The other left last night, because she couldn't get on with my mother-in-law."

"They never can!" said Miss Vernon.

"Anyhow, Herbert doesn't think it ladylike for me to do housework."

Madge Vernon scoffed at the idea.

"Ladylike! Oh, this suburban snobbishness! How I hate the damn thing! Forgive my bad language, won't you?"

"I like it," said Clare.

Miss Vernon continued her cross-examination.

"Don't you even make your own bed? It's awfully healthy to turn a mattress and throw the pillows about."

"Herbert objects to my making beds," said Clare.

"Don't you make the puddings or help in the washing up?"

"Herbert objects to my going into the kitchen," said Clare.

"Don't you ever break a few plates?"

Clare smiled at her queer question.

"No, why should I?"

"There's nothing like breaking things to relieve one's pent-up emotions," said Miss Vernon, with an air of profound knowledge.

"The only thing I have broken lately is something—here," said Clare, putting her hand to her heart.

Miss Vernon was scornful.

"Oh, rubbish! The heart is unbreakable, my dear. Now, heads are much easier to crack."

"I think mine is getting cracked, too," said Clare.

She put her hands to her head, as though it were grievously cracked.

Madge Vernon stared at her frankly and thoughtfully.

"Look here," she said, after a little silence, "I tell you what *you* want. It's a baby. Why don't you have one?"

"Herbert can't afford it," said Clare. Madge Vernon raised her hands.

"Stuff and nonsense!" she said.

"Besides," said Clare in a matter-of-fact way, "they don't make flats big enough for babies in Intellectual Mansions."

Madge Vernon looked round the room, and frowned angrily.

"No, that's true. There's no place to keep a perambulator. Oh, these jerry builders! Immoral devils!"

There was a silence between the two women. Both of them seemed deep in thought.

Then presently Clare said: "I feel as if something were going to happen; as if something must happen or break."

"About time, my dear," said Madge. "How long have you been married?"

"Eight years," said Clare, in a casual way. Madge Vernon whistled with a long-drawn note of ominous meaning.

"The Eighth Year, eh?"

"Yes, it's our eighth year of marriage."

"That's bad," said Madge. "The Eighth Year! You will have to be very careful, Clare."

Clare was startled. "What do you mean?" she asked.

"Haven't you heard?" said Miss Vernon.

"Heard what?"

"I thought everybody knew."

"Knew what?" asked Clare anxiously.

Madge Vernon looked at her in a pitying way.

"It's in the evidence on the Royal Commission on Divorce."

"What is?"

"About the Eighth Year."

"What about it?" asked Clare. She was beginning to feel annoyed. What was Madge hiding from her?

"Why," said Madge, "about it being the fatal year in marriage."

"The fatal year?"

The girl leaned forward in her chair and said in a solemn way:

"There are more divorces begun in the Eighth Year than in any other period."

Clare Heywood was scared.

"Good gracious!" she said, in a kind of whisper.

"It's a psychological fact," said Madge. "I work it out in this way. In the first and second years a wife is absorbed in the experiment of marriage and in the sentimental phase of love. In the third and fourth years she begins to study her husband and to find him out. In the fifth and sixth years, having found him out completely, she makes a working compromise with life and tries to make the best of it. In the seventh and eighth years she begins to find out herself, and then——"

"And then?" asked Clare, very anxiously.

Clare Heywood was profoundly disturbed.

"Well, then," said Madge, "there is the devil to pay!"

"Dear God!" she cried.

"You see, it's like this. If a woman has no child she gets bored.... She can't help getting bored, poor soul. Her husband is so devoted to her that he provides her with every opportunity for getting bored—extra servants, extra little luxuries, and what he calls a beautiful little home. Ugh!" She stared round the room and made a face.

"He is so intent on this that he nearly works himself to death. Comes home with business thoughts in his head. Doesn't notice his wife's wistful eyes, and probably dozes off to sleep after supper. Isn't that so?"

"Yes," said Clare. "Horribly so."

"Well, then, having got bored, she gets emotional. Of course the husband doesn't notice that either. *He's* not emotional. He is only wondering how to make both ends meet. But when his wife begins to get emotional, when she feels that something has broken here" (she put her hand to her heart), "when she feels like crying at unexpected moments and laughing at the wrong time, why then——"

"What?" asked Clare.

"Why, then, it's about time the husband began to notice things, or things will begin to happen to his wife which he won't jolly well like. That's all!"

Clare Heywood searched her friend's face with hungry eyes.

"Why, what will his wife do?"

"Well, there are various alternatives. She either takes to religion——"

"Ah!" said Clare, flushing a little.

"Or to drink——"

"Oh, no!" said Clare, shuddering a little.

"Or to some other kind of man," said Madge very calmly.

Clare Heywood was agitated and alarmed.

"How do you know these things?" she asked.

"Oh, I've studied 'em," said Madge Vernon cheerfully. "Of course there's always another alternative."

"What's that?" asked Clare eagerly.

"Work," said Madge Vernon solemnly.

"What kind of work?"

"Oh, any kind, so long as it's absorbing and satisfying. Personally I like breaking things. One must always begin by breaking before one begins building. But it's very exciting."

"It must be terribly exciting."

"For instance," said Madge, laughing quietly, "it's good to hear a pane of glass go crack."

"How does it make you feel?" asked Clare Heywood.

"Oh," said Madge, "it gives one a jolly feeling down the spine. You should try it."

"I daren't," said Clare.

"It would do you a lot of good. It would get rid of your megrims. Besides, it's in a good cause."

"I am not so sure of that," said Clare.

"It's in the cause of woman's liberty. It's in the cause of all these suburban wives imprisoned in these stuffy little homes. It lets in God's fresh air."

Clare rose and moved about the room. "It's very stuffy in here," she said. "It's stifling." At this moment Mollie came in the room again, and smiled across at her mistress, saying: "Mr. Bradshaw to see you, ma'am."

Clare was obviously agitated. She showed signs of embarrassment, and her voice trembled when she said:

"Tell him—tell him I'm engaged."

"He says he must see you—on business," said Mollie, lingering at the door.

"On business?"

"That's what my young man says when he whistles up the tube," said Mollie.

Madge Vernon looked at her friend and said rather "meaningly": "Don't you *want* to see him? If so I shouldn't if I were you."

"Oh, yes," said Clare, trying to appear quite cool. "If it's on business."

"Very well, ma'am," said Mollie. As she left the room she said under her breath: "I thought you would."

"Do you have business relations with Mr. Bradshaw?" asked Madge Vernon.

"Yes," said Clare; "no.... In a sort of way."

"I thought he was a novelist," said Madge.

"So he is."

"Dangerous fellows, novelists."

"Hush!" said Clare. "He might hear you."

"If it's on business I must go, I suppose," said Madge Vernon, rising from her chair.

"No, don't go; stay!" said Clare, speaking with strange excitement.

As soon as she had uttered the words the visitor, Gerald Bradshaw, came in.

He was a handsome, "artistic" looking man, with longish brown hair and a vandyke beard. He was dressed in a brown suit, with a big brown silk tie. He came forward in a graceful way, perfectly at ease, and with a charming manner.

"How do you do, Mrs. Heywood?"

"I *must* be going," said Madge. "Good-by, dear."

"Oh, *do* stay," whispered Clare.

"Impossible. I have to speak to-night."

Although Madge Vernon had ignored the artist, he smiled at her and said:

"Don't you speak by day as a rule?"

"Not until I am spoken to.... Good-night, Clare."

"Well, if you must be going—" said Clare uneasily.

Madge Vernon stood for a moment at the door and smiled back at her friend. "You will remember, won't you?"

"What?"

"The Eighth Year," said Madge. With that parting shot she whisked out of the room.

Gerald Bradshaw breathed a sigh of relief. Then he went across to Clare and kissed her hands.

"I can't stand that creature. A she-devil!"

"She is my friend," said Clare.

"I am sorry to hear it," said Gerald Bradshaw.

Clare Heywood drooped her eyelashes before his bold, smiling gaze.

"Why did you come again?" she asked. "I told you not to come."

"That is why I came. May I smoke?"

He lit a cigarette before he had received he permission, and after a whiff or two said:

"Is the good man at the club?"

"You know he is at the club," said Clare. "True. That is another reason why I came. Clare Heywood's face flushed and her voice trembled a little.

"Gerald, if you had any respect for me——

"Respect is a foolish word," said Gerald Bradshaw. "Hopelessly old-fashioned. Now adays men and women like or dislike, hate or love."

"I think I hate you," said Clare in a low voice.

Gerald smiled at her.

"No, you don't. You are a little frightened of me. That is all."

The woman laughed nervously, but there was a look of fear in her eyes.

"Why should I be frightened of you?"

"Because I tell you the truth. I don't keep up the foolish old pretences by which men and women hide themselves from each other. You cannot hide from me, Clare."

"You seem to strip my soul bare," said Clare and when the man laughed at her she said: "Yes, I am frightened of you."

"It is because you are like all suburban women," said Gerald, "brought up in this environment of hypocritical virtue and false sentiment. You are frightened at the verities of life."

Clare Heywood gave a deep, quivering sigh. "Life is a tragic thing, Gerald," she said. "Life is a jolly thing if one makes the best of it, if one fulfils one's own nature."

"One's own nature is generally bad."

"Never mind," said Gerald cheerfully. "It is one's own. Bad or good, it must find expression instead of being smothered or strangled. Life is tragic only to those who are afraid of it. Don't be afraid, Clare. Do the things you want to do."

"There is nothing I want to do," said Clare wearily. "Nothing except to find peace."

"Exactly. Peace. How can you find peace, my poor Clare, in this stuffy life of yours—in this daily denial of your own nature? There are heaps of things you want."

Clare laughed again, in a mirthless way. "How do you know?" she asked.

"Of course I know. Shall I tell you?"

"I think I would rather you didn't," said Clare.

"I will tell you," said the man. "Liberty is one of them."

"Liberty is a vague word."

"Liberty for your soul," said Gerald.

"Herbert objects to my having a soul."

"Liberty for that beating heart of yours, Clare."

The woman put both hands to her heart.

"Yes, it beats, and beats."

"You want to escape, Clare."

"Escape?"

She seemed frightened at that word. She whispered it.

"Escape from the deadening influence of domestic dulness."

"I can't deny the dulness," said Clare.

"You want adventure. Your heart is seeking adventure. You know it. You know that I am telling you the truth."

As the man spoke he came closer to her, and with his hands in his pockets stood in front of her, staring into her eyes.

"You make me afraid," said Clare. All the color had faded out of her face and she was dead white.

"You need not be afraid, Clare. The love of a man for a woman is not a terrifying thing. It is a good thing. Good as life."

He took her by the wrists and held them tight.

"Gerald!" said Clare. "For God's sake.... I have a husband."

"He bores you," said the man. "He is your husband but not your mate. No woman finds peace until she finds her mate. It is the same with a man."

"I will not listen to you. You make me feel a bad woman!"

She wrenched her hands free and moved toward the bell.

Gerald Bradshaw laughed quietly. He seemed amused at this woman's fear. He seemed masterful, sure of his power over her.

"You know that you must be my mate. If not to-day, to-morrow. If not to-morrow, the next day. I will wait for you, Clare."

Clare had shrunk back to the wall now, and touched the electric bell.

"You have no pity for me," she said. "You play on my weakness."

"Fear makes you strong to resist," said the man. "But love is stronger than fear."

He followed her across the room to where she stood crouching against the wall like a hunted thing.

"Don't come so close to me," she said.

"What on earth have you rung the bell for?" asked the man.

"Because I ought not to be alone with you."

They stood looking into each other's eyes. Then Clare moved quickly toward the sofa as Mollie came in.

"Oh, Mollie," said Clare, trying to steady her voice, "ask Mrs. Heywood to come in, will you? Tell her Mr. Bradshaw is here."

"Yes, ma'am," said Mollie. "But she knows that already."

"Take my message, please," said her mistress.

"I was going to, ma'am," said Mollie, and she added in an undertone, as she left the room, "Strange as it may appear."

Gerald laughed quite light-heartedly.

"Yes, you have won the trick this time. But I hold the trump cards, Clare; and I am very lucky, as a rule. I have a gambler's luck. Of course if the old lady comes in I shan't stay. She hates me like poison, and I can't be polite to her. Insincerity is not one of my vices. Good-night, dear heart. I will come to you in your dreams."

As he spoke this word, which brought a flush again to Clare Heywood's face, Mrs. Hey-wood, her mother-in-law, came in. She glanced from one to the other suspiciously.

Gerald Bradshaw was not in the least abashed by her stern face.

"How do you do, Mrs. Heywood? I was just going. I hope I have not disturbed you?"

Mrs. Heywood answered him in a "distant" manner:

"Not in the least."

"I am glad," he said. "I will let myself out. Don't trouble."

At that moment there was a noise in the hall, and Clare raised her head and listened.

"I think I hear another visitor," she said.

"In that ease I had better wait a moment," said Gerald. "The halls of these flats are not cut out for two people at a time. I will light another cigarette if I may."

"I thought I heard a latchkey," said Mrs. Heywood. "Surely it can't he Herbert back so early?"

"No, it can't be," said Clare.

Gerald spoke more to himself than to the ladies:

"I hope not."

They were all silent when Herbert Heywood came in quietly.

"I didn't go to the club after all," he said. Then he saw Gerald Bradshaw, and his mouth hardened a little as he said, "Oh!... How do?"

"How are you?" asked Gerald, in his cool way.

"Been here long?" asked Herbert.

"Long enough for a pleasant talk with your wife."

"Going now?"

"Yes. We have finished our chat. Goodnight. I can find my way out blindfolded. All these flats are the same. Rather convenient, don't you think?"

He turned to Clare and smiled.

"*Au revoir*, Mrs. Heywood."

She did not answer him, and he went out jauntily. A few moments later they heard the front door shut.

"What the devil does he come here for?" growled Herbert rather sulkily.

Clare ignored the question.

"Why are you home so early?"

"Yes, dear, why didn't you go to the club?" asked Mrs. Heywood.

Herbert looked rather embarrassed.

"Oh, I don't know. I felt a bit off. Besides——"

"What, dear?" asked his mother.

"I thought Clare was feeling a bit lonely to-night. Perhaps I was mistaken."

"I am often lonely," said Clare. "Even when you are at home."

"Aren't you *glad* I have come back?" asked Herbert.

"Why do you ask me?"

"I should be glad if you were glad." Clare's husband became slightly sentimental as he looked at her.

"I have been thinking it *is* rather rotten to go *off* to the club and leave you here alone," he said.

Mrs. Heywood was delighted with these words.

"Oh, you dear boy! How unselfish of you!"

"I try to be," said Herbert.

"I am sure you are the very soul of unselfishness, Herbert, dear," said the fond mother.

"Thanks, mother."

He looked rather anxiously at Clare, and said—

"Don't you think we might have a pleasant evening for once?"

"Oh, that would be delightful!" said Mrs. Heywood.

"Eh, Clare?"

"How do you mean?" said Clare.

"Like we used to in the old days? Some music, and that sort of thing."

"I am sure that will be *very* nice," said Mrs. Heywood.

"Eh, Clare?" said Herbert.

"If you like," said Clare.

"Wait till I have got my boots off." He spoke in a rather honeyed voice to his wife.

"Do you happen to know where my slippers are, darling?"

"I haven't the least idea," said Clare.

Herbert seemed nettled at this answer.

"In the old days you used to warm them for me," he said.

"Did I?" said Clare. "I have forgotten. It was a long time ago."

"Eight years."

At these words Clare looked over to her husband in a peculiar way.

"Yes," she said. "It is our eighth year."

"Here are your slippers, dear," said Mrs. Hey wood.

"Oh, thanks, mother. *You* don't forget."

There was silence while he took off his boots. Clare sat with her hands in her lap, staring at the carpet. Once or twice her mother-in-law glanced at her anxiously.

"Won't you play something, Clare?" said the old lady, after a little while.

"If you like," said Clare.

Herbert resumed his cheerful note.

"Yes, let's have a jolly evening. Perhaps I will sing a song presently."

"Oh, do, dear!" said Mrs. Heywood.

"Gad, it's a long time since I sang 'John Peel'!"

Clare looked rather anxious and perturbed.

"The walls of this flat are rather thin," she said. "The neighbors might not like it."

"Oh, confound the neighbors!" said Herbert.

"I will do some knitting while you two dears play and sing," said the old lady.

She fetched her knitting from a black silk bag on one of the little tables, and took a chair near the fireplace. Clare Heywood went to the music-stool and turned over some music listlessly. She did not seem to find anything which appealed to her.

Her husband settled himself down in an arm-chair and loaded his pipe.

"Play something bright, Clare," he said.

"All my music sounds melancholy when I play it," said Clare.

"What, rag-time?"

"Even rag-time. Rag-time worst of all."

Yet she began to play softly one of Chopin's preludes, in a dreamy way.

"Tell me when you want me to sing," said Herbert.

"I will," said Clare.

There was silence for a little while, except for Clare's dream-music. Mrs. Heywood dozed over her knitting, and her head nodded on her chest. Presently Herbert rose from his chair and touched the electric bell. A moment later Mollie came in.

"Yes?" asked Mollie.

Herbert spoke quietly so that he should not interrupt his wife's music.

"Bring me *The Financial Times*, Mollie. It's in my study."

"Yes, sir," said Mollie.

She brought the paper and left the room again. There was another silence, except for the soft notes of the music. Herbert turned over the pages of *The Financial Times*, and yawned a little, and then let the paper drop. His head nodded and then lolled sideways. In a little while he was as fast asleep as his mother, and snored, quietly at first, then quite loudly.

Clare stopped playing, and looked over the music-rest with a strange, tragic smile at her husband and her mother-in-law. She rose from the piano-stool, and put her hands to her head, and then at her throat, breathing quickly and jerkily, as though she were being stifled.

"A jolly evening!" she exclaimed in a whisper. "Oh, God!"

She stared round the room, with rather wild eyes.

"It is stuffy here. It is stifling."

She moved toward the piano again, with her hands pressed against her bosom.

"I feel that something *must* happen. Something *must* break."

She took up a large china vase from the piano, moved slowly toward the window, hesitated for a moment, looked round at her sleeping husband, and then hurled the vase straight through the window. It made an appalling noise of breaking glass.

Herbert Heywood jumped up from his seat as though he had been shot.

"Good God!" he said. "What the devil!——"

Mrs. Heywood was equally startled. She sat up in her chair as though an earthquake had shaken the house.

"Good gracious! Whatever in the world——-"

At the same moment Mollie opened the door.

"Good 'eavins, ma'am!" she cried. "Whatever 'as 'appened?"

Clare Heywood answered very quietly:

"I think something must have broken," she said.

Then she gave a queer, strident laugh.

CHAPTER II

MRS. Heywood was arranging the drawingroom for an evening At Home, dusting the mantelshelf and some of the ornaments with a little hand broom. There were refreshments on a side table. Mollie was trying to make the fire burn up. Every now and then a gust of smoke blew down the chimney. Clare was sitting listlessly in a low chair near the French window, with a book on her lap, but she was not reading.

"Drat the fire," said Mollie, with her head in the fireplace.

"For goodness' sake, Mollie, stop it smoking like that!" said Mrs. Heywood. "It's no use my dusting the room."

"The devil is in the chimney, it strikes me," said Mollie.

Mrs. Heywood expressed her sense of exasperation.

"It's a funny thing that every time your mistress gives an At Home you are always behindhand with your work."

Mollie expressed her feelings in the firegrate.

"It's a funny thing people can't mind their own business."

"What did you say, Mollie?" asked Mrs. Heywood sharply.

"I said that the fire hasn't gone right since the window was broke. Them Suffragettes have a lot to answer for."

"I cannot understand how it *did* get broken," said Mrs. Heywood. "I almost suspect that woman, Miss Vernon."

Clare looked up and spoke irritably.

"Nonsense, mother!"

"It's no use saying nonsense, Clare," said Mrs. Heywood, even more irritably. "You know perfectly well that Miss Vernon is a most dangerous woman."

"Well, she didn't break our window, anyhow," said Clare, rather doggedly.

"How do you know that? It is still a perfect mystery."

"Don't be absurd, mother. How did the vase get through the window?"

Mrs. Heywood was baffled for an answer.

"Ah, that is most perplexing."

"Well, leave it at that," said Clare.

Mollie was still wrestling with the mysteries of light and heat.

"If it doesn't burn now," she said, "I won't lay another finger on it—At Home or no At Home."

She seized the dustpan and broom and, with a hot face, marched out of the room.

Clare pressed her forehead with the tips of her fingers.

"I wish to Heaven there were no such things as At Homes," she said wearily. "Oh, how they bore me!"

"You used to like them well enough," said Mrs. Heywood.

"I have grown out of them. I have grown out of so many things. It is as if my life had shrunk in the wash."

"Nothing seems to please you now," said the old lady. "Don't you care for your friends any longer?"

"Friends? Those tittle-tattling women, with their empty-headed husbands?"

Mrs. Heywood was silent for a moment. Then she spoke bitterly.

"Do you think Herbert is empty-headed?"

"Oh, we won't get personal, mother," said Clare. "And we won't quarrel, if you don't mind."

Mrs. Heywood's lips tightened.

"I am afraid we shall if you go on like this."

"Like what?" asked Clare.

"Hush!" said the old lady. "Here comes Herbert."

Herbert came in quickly, and raised his eyebrows after a glance at his wife.

"Good Lord, Clare! Aren't you dressed yet?"

"There's plenty of time, isn't there?" said Clare.

"No, there isn't," said Herbert. "You know some of the guests will arrive before eight o'clock."

Clare looked up at the clock.

"It's only six now."

"Besides," said Herbert, "I want you to look your best to-night. Edward Hargreaves is coming, with his wife."

"What has that got to do with it?"

"Everything," said Herbert. "He is second cousin to one of my directors. It is essential that you should make a good impression."

"You told me once that he was a complete ass," said Clare.

"So he is."

"Well, then," said Clare, quietly but firmly, "I decline to make a good impression on him."

"I must ask you to obey my wishes," said Herbert.

Clare had rebellion in her eyes.

"I have obeyed you for seven years. It is now the Eighth Year."

Herbert did not hear his wife's remark. He was looking round the room with an air of extreme annoyance.

"Well, I'm blowed!" he exclaimed.

"What's the matter, dear?" asked Mrs. Hey-wood anxiously.

"You haven't even taken the trouble to buy some flowers," said Herbert.

"I left that to Clare," said the old lady.

"Haven't you done so, Clare?"

"No," said Clare. "I can't bear flowers in this room. They droop so quickly."

Herbert was quite angry.

"I insist upon having some flowers. The place looks like a barn without them. What will our visitors say?"

"Stupid things, as usual," said Clare quietly.

"I must go out and get some myself, I suppose," said Herbert, with the air of a martyr.

"Can't you send Mollie, dear?" asked Mrs. Heywood.

"Mollie is cutting sandwiches. The girl is overwhelmed with work. And—Oh, my stars!"

His mother was alarmed by this sudden cry of dismay.

"Now what is the matter, dear?"

"There's no whisky in the decanter."

"No whisky?"

"Clare," said Herbert, appealing to his wife, "there's not a drop of whisky left."

"Well, *I* didn't drink it," said Clare. "You finished it the other night with one of your club friends."

"So we did. Dash it!"

"Don't be irritable, dear," said Mrs. Heywood.

"Irritable! Isn't it enough to make a saint irritable? These things always happen on our At Home nights. Nobody seems to have any forethought. Every blessed thing seems to go wrong."

"That is why I wish one could abolish the institution," said Clare.

"What institution?"

"At Homes."

"Don't talk rubbish, Clare," said Herbert angrily; "you know I have them for *your* sake."

Clare laughed bitterly, as though she had heard a rather painful joke.

"For my sake! Oh, that is good!"

Herbert was distracted by a new cause of grievance as a tremendous puff of smoke came out of the fire-grate.

"What in the name of a thousand devils——"

"It's that awful fire again!" cried Mrs. Hey-wood. "These flats seem to have no chimneys."

"It's nothing to do with the flat," said Herbert. "It's that fool Mollie. The girl doesn't know how to light a decent fire!"

He rang the bell furiously, keeping his finger on the electric knob.

"The creature has absolutely nothing to do, and what she does she spoils."

Mollie came in with a look of mutiny on her face.

"Look at that fire," said Herbert fiercely.

"I am looking at it," said Mollie.

"Why don't you do your work properly? See to the beastly thing, can't you?"

Mollie folded her arms and spoke firmly.

"If you please, sir, wild horses won't make me touch it again."

"It's not a question of horse-power," said Herbert. "Go and get an old newspaper and hold it in front of the bars."

"I am just in the middle of the sandwiches," said Mollie.

"Well, get out of them, then," said Herbert.

Mollie delivered her usual ultimatum.

"If you please, sir, I beg to give a month's notice."

"Bosh!" said Herbert.

"Bosh indeed!" cried Mollie. "We'll see if it's bosh! If you want any sandwiches for your precious visitors you can cut 'em yourself."

With this challenge she went out of the room and slammed the door behind her.

Herbert breathed deeply, and after a moment's struggle in his soul spoke mildly.

"Mother, go and pacify the fool, will you?"

"She is very obstinate," said Mrs. Heywood.

"All women are obstinate."

Suddenly the man's self-restraint broke down and he became excited.

"Bribe her, promise her a rise in wages, but for God's sake see that she cuts the sandwiches. We don't want to be made fools of before our guests."

"Very well, dear," said Mrs. Heywood. She hesitated for a moment at the door, and before going out said: "But Mollie can be very violent at times."

For a little while there was silence between the husband and wife. Then Herbert spoke rather sternly.

"Clare, are you or are you not going to get dressed?"

"I shall get dressed in good time," said Clare quietly, "when I think fit. Surely you don't want to dictate to me about *that?*"

"Surely," said Herbert, "you can see how awkward it will be if any of our people arrive and find you unprepared for them?"

Clare gave a long, weary sigh.

"Oh, I *am* prepared for them. I have been trying to prepare myself all day for the ordeal of, them."

"The ordeal? What the dickens do you mean?"

"I am prepared for Mrs. Atkinson Brown, who, when she takes off her hat in the bedroom, will ask me whether I am suited and whether I am expecting."

"For goodness' sake don't be coarse, Clare," said Herbert.

"It's Mrs. Atkinson Brown who is coarse," said Clare. "And I am prepared for Mr. Atkinson Brown, who will say that it is horrible weather for this time of year, and that business has been the very devil since there has been a Radical Government, and that these outrageous women who are breaking windows ought to be whipped. Oh, I could tell you everything that everybody is going to say. I have heard it over and over again."

"It does not seem to make much effect on you," said Herbert. "Especially that part about breaking windows."

Clare smiled.

"So you have guessed, have you?"

"I knew at once by the look on your face."

"I thought you agreed with your mother that some Suffragette must have flung a stone from the outside."

"I hid the truth from mother," said Herbert. "She would think you were mad. What on earth made you do it? *Were* you mad or what?"

Clare brushed her hair back from her forehead.

"Sometimes I used to think I was going a little mad. But now I know what is the matter with me."

Herbert spoke more tenderly.

"What *is* the matter, Clare? If it is a question of a doctor——"

"It's the Eighth Year," said Clare.

"The Eighth Year?"

"Yes, that's what is the matter with me."

"What on earth do you mean?" asked Herbert.

"Why, don't you know? It was Madge Vernon who told me."

"Told you what?"

"She seemed to think that everybody knew."

"Knew what?" asked Herbert, exasperated beyond all patience.

"About the Eighth Year."

"What about it?"

"It's well known, she says, that the Eighth Year is the most dangerous one in marriage. It is then that the pull comes, when the wife has found out her husband."

"Found out her husband?"

"And found out herself."

Herbert spoke roughly. He was not in a mood for such mysteries.

"Look here," he said. "I can't listen to all this nonsense. Go and dress yourself."

"I want to talk to you, Herbert," said Clare very earnestly. "I must talk to you before it's too late."

"It's too late now," said Herbert. "Halfpast six. I must fetch that whisky and buy a few flowers. I shall have to put on my boots again and splash about in the mud in these trousers. Confound it!"

"Before you go you must listen, Herbert," said Clare, with a sign of emotion. "Perhaps you won't have another chance."

"Thank Heaven for that."

"When I broke that window something else broke."

"One of my best vases," said Herbert with sarcasm.

"I think something in my own nature broke too. My spirit has broken out of this narrow, deadening little life of ours, out of the smug snobbishness and stupidity which for so long kept me prisoner, out of the belief that the latest sentimental novel, the latest romantic play, the latest bit of tittle-tattle from my neighbors might satisfy my heart and brain. When I broke that window I let a little fresh air into the stifling atmosphere of this flat, where I have been mewed up without work, without any kind of honest interest, without any kind of food for my brain or soul."

Herbert stared at his wife, and made an impatient gesture.

"If you want work, why don't you attend to your domestic duties?"

"I have no domestic duties," said Clare. "That is the trouble."

Herbert laughed in an unpleasant way.

"Why, you haven't even bought any flowers to decorate your home! Isn't that a domestic duty?"

Clare answered him quickly, excitedly.

"It's just a part of the same old hypocrisy of keeping up appearances. You know you don't care for flowers in themselves, except as they help to make a show. You want to impress our guests. You want to keep up the old illusion of the woman's hand in the home. The woman's touch. Isn't that it?"

"Yes, I do want to keep up that illusion," said Herbert; "and by God, I find it very hard! You say you want an object in life. Isn't your husband an object?"

Clare looked at him with a queer, pitiful smile.

"Yes, he is," she said slowly.

"Well, what more do you want?"

"Lots more. A woman's life is not centered for ever in one man."

"It ought to be," said Herbert. "If you had any religious principles——"

"Oh," said Clare sharply, "but you object to my religion!"

"Well, of course I mean in moderation."

"You have starved me, Herbert, and oh, I am so hungry!"

Herbert answered her airily.

"Well, there will be light refreshments later."

"Yes, that is worthy of you," cried Clare. "That is your sense of humor! You have starved my soul and starved my heart and you offer me—sandwiches. I am hungry for life and you offer me—the latest novel."

Herbert paced up and down the room. He was losing control of his temper.

"That is the reward for all my devotion!" he said. "Don't I drudge in the city every day to keep you in comfort?"

"I don't want comfort!" said Clare.

"Don't I toil so that you may have pretty frocks?"

"I don't want pretty frocks."

"Don't I scrape and scheme to buy you little luxuries?"

"I don't want little luxuries," said Clare.

"Is there anything within my means that you haven't got?"

Clare looked at him in a peculiar way, and answered quietly—

"I haven't a child," she said.

"Oh, Lord," said Herbert uneasily. "Whose fault is that? Besides, modern life in small flats is not cut out for children."

"And modern life in small flats," said Clare, "is not cut out for wives."

"It isn't my fault," said Herbert. "I am not the architect—either of fate or flats."

"No, it isn't your fault, Herbert. You can't help your character. It isn't your fault that when you come home from the city you fall asleep after dinner. It isn't your fault that when you go to the club I sit at home with my hands in my lap, thinking and brooding. It isn't your fault that your mother and I get on each other's nerves. It isn't your fault that you and I have grown out of each other, that we bore each other and have nothing to say to each other—except when we quarrel."

"Well, then," said Herbert, "whose fault is it?"

"I don't know," said Clare. "I suppose it's a fault of the system, which is spoiling thousands of marriages just like ours. It's the fault which is found out—in the Eighth Year."

"Oh, curse the Eighth Year," said Herbert violently. "What is that bee you have got in your bonnet?"

"It's a bee which keeps buzzing in my brain. It's a little bee which whispers queer words to me—tempting words. It says you must break away from the system or the system will break you. You must find a way of escape or die. You must do it quickly, now, to-night, or it will be too late. Herbert, a hungry woman will do desperate things to satisfy her appetite, and I am hungry for some stronger emotion than I can find within these four walls. I am hungry for love, hungry for work, hungry for life. If you can't give it to me, I must find it elsewhere."

"Clare," said Herbert, with deliberate self-restraint, "I must again remind you that time is getting on and you are not yet dressed. In a little while our guests will be here. I hope you don't mean to hold me up to the contempt of my friends. I at least have some sense of duty.... I am going to fetch the whisky." As he strode toward the door he started back at the noise of breaking china.

"What's that?" asked Clare.

"God knows," said Herbert. "I expect mother has broken a window."

The words were hardly out of his mouth before Mrs. Heywood came in in a state of great agitation.

"Herbert, I must really ask you to come into the kitchen."

"What's the matter now?" asked Herbert, prepared for the worst.

"Mollie has deliberately broken our best coffee-pot."

Herbert stared at his wife.

"Didn't I tell you so!" he said.

"Why has she broken the coffee-pot?" asked Clare.

"She was most insolent," said Mrs. Heywood, "and said my interference got on her nerves."

"Well, even a servant *has* nerves," said Clare.

"But it was the *best* coffee-pot, Clare. Surely you are not going to take it so calmly?"

"Like mistress like maid!" said Herbert. "Oh, my hat! Why on earth did I marry?"

"Don't you think you had better fetch the whisky?" said Clare gently.

Herbert became excited again.

"I have been trying to fetch the whisky for the last half hour. There is a conspiracy against it. Confound it, I *will* fetch the whisky."

He strode to the door, as though he would get the whisky or die in the attempt.

"I think you ought to speak to Mollie first," said Mrs. Heywood.

Herbert raised his hands above his head.

"Damn Mollie!" he shouted wildly. Then he strode out of the room. "Damn everything!"

"Poor dear," said Mrs. Heywood. "I wish he didn't get so worried."

"Clare, won't you come and speak to Mollie?"

"Haven't you spoken to her?" asked Clare wearily.

"I am always speaking to her."

"*Poor* Mollie!" said Clare.

Mrs. Heywood was hurt at the tone of pity. She flushed a little and then turned to her daughter-in-law with reproachful eyes.

"I am an old woman, Clare, and the mother of your husband. Because my position forces me to live in this flat, I do not think you ought to insult me."

"I'm sorry," said Clare with sincerity.

"Mollie is right. We all get on each other's nerves. It can't be helped, I suppose. It's part of the system."

"I can't help being your mother-in-law, Clare."

"No, it can't he helped," said Clare.

Mrs. Heywood came close to her and touched her hand.

"You think I do not understand. You think you are the only one who has any grievance."

"Oh, no!" said Clare. "I am not so egotistical."

Mrs. Heywood smoothed down her dress with trembling hands.

"You think I haven't been watching you all these years. I have watched you so that I know your thoughts behind those brooding eyes, Clare. I know all that you have been thinking and suffering, so that sometimes you hate me, so that my very presence here in the room with you makes you wish to cry out, to shriek, because I am your mother-in-law, and the mother of your husband. The husband always loves his mother best, and the wife always knows it. That is the eternal tragedy of the mother-in-law. Because she is hated by the wife of her son, and is an intruder in her home. I know that because I too suffered from a mother-in-law. Do you think I would stay here an hour unless I was forced to stay, for a shelter above my old head, for some home in which I wait to die? But while I wait I watch... and I know that you have reached a dangerous stage in a woman's life, when she may do any rash thing. Clare, I pray every night that you may pass that stage in life without doing anything—rash. This time always comes in marriage, it comes——"

"In the Eighth Year?" asked Clare eagerly. "Somewhere about then."

"Ah! I thought so."

"It came to me, my dear."

"And did *you* do anything rash?"

Mrs. Heywood hesitated a moment before replying.

"I gave birth to Herbert," she said.

"Good Heavens!" said Clare.

"It saved me from breaking——"

"Windows, mother?"

"No, my own and my husband's heart," said Mrs. Heywood. "Well, I will go and speak to Mollie again. Goodness knows how we shall get coffee to-night."

She went out of the room with her head shaking a little after this scene of emotion.

Clare spoke to herself aloud. She had her hands up to her throat.

"I don't want coffee to-night. I want stronger drink. I want to get drunk with liberty of life."

Suddenly there was a noise at the window and the woman looked up, startled, and cried, "Who is there?"

Gerald Bradshaw appeared at the open French window leading on to the balcony, and he spoke through the window.

"It is I, Clare? Are you alone?"

Clare had risen from her chair at the sound of his voice, and her face became very pale.

"Gerald... How did you come there?"

Gerald Bradshaw laughed in his lighthearted way.

"I stepped over the bar that divides our balconies. It was quite easy. It was as easy as it will be to cross the bar that divides you and me, Clare."

Clare spoke in a frightened voice.

"Why do you come here, at this hour?"

"Why do I ever come?" asked Gerald Bradshaw.

"I don't know."

"It's because I want you. I want you badly to-night, Clare. I can't wait for you any longer."

Clare spoke pleadingly.

"Gerald... go away... it's so dangerous... I daren't listen to you."

"I want you to listen," said Gerald Bradshaw.

"Go away... I implore you to go away."

He laughed at her. He seemed very much amused.

"Not before I have said what I want to say."

"Say it quickly," said Clare. "Quickly!"

"There's time enough," said Bradshaw. "This is what I want to say. You are a lonely woman and I am a lonely man, and only an iron bar divides us. It's the iron bar of convention, of insincerity, of superstition. It seems so difficult to cross. But you see one step is enough. I want you to take that step—to-night."

Clare answered him in a whisper.

"Go away!"

"I am hungry for you," said Bradshaw, with a thrill in his voice. "I am hungry for your love. And you are hungry for me. I have seen it in your eyes. You have the look of a famished woman. Famished for love. Famished for comradeship."

Clare raised her hands despairingly.

"If you have any pity, go away."

"I have no pity. Because pity is weakness, and I hate weakness."

"You are brutal," said Clare.

He laughed at her. He seemed to like those words.

"Yes, I have the brutality of manhood. Man is a brute, and woman likes the brute in him because that is his nature, and woman wants the natural man. That is why you want me, Clare. You can't deny it."

Clare protested feebly.

"I do deny it. I *must* deny it."

"It's a funny thing," said Gerald Bradshaw. "Between you and me there is a queer spell, Clare. I was conscious of it when I first met you. Something in you calls to me. Something in me calls to you. It is the call of the wild."

Clare was scared now. These words seemed to make her heart beat to a strange tune.

"What do you mean?" she said.

"It is the call of the untamed creature. Both you and I are untamed. We both have the spirit of the woods. I am Pan. You are a wood nymph, imprisoned in a cage, upholstered by maple, on the hire system."

"What do you want with me?" asked Clare. It was clear that he was tempting her.

"I want to play with you, like Pan played. You and I will hear the pipes of Pan to-night—the wild nature music."

"To-night?"

"To-night. I have waited too long for you, and now I'm impatient. I am alone in my flat waiting for you. I ask you to keep me company, not to-night only, but until we tire of each other, until perhaps we hate each other. Who knows?"

"Oh, God!" said Clare. She moaned out the words in a pitiful way.

"You have only to slip down one flight of stairs and steal up another, and you will find me at the door with a welcome. It will need just a little care to escape from your prison. You must slip on your hat and cloak as though you were going round to church, and then come to me, to me, Clare! Only a wall will divide you from this flat, but you will be a world away. For you will have escaped from this upholstered cage into a little world of liberty. Into a little world of love, Clare. Say you will come!"

"Oh, God!" moaned Clare.

"You will come?"

"Are you the Devil that you tempt me?" said Clare.

Gerald gave a triumphant little laugh.

"You will come! Clare, my sweetheart, I know you will come, for your spirit is ready for me."

As he spoke these words there was the sound of a bell ringing through the flat, and the noise of it struck terror into Clare Heywood.

"Go away," she whispered. "For God's sake go! Some one is ringing."

"I will cross the bar again," said Bradshaw. "But I shall be waiting at the door. You will not be very long, little one?"

Clare sank down with her face in her hands. And Gerald stole away from the window just as Mollie showed in Madge Vernon.

"It's our At Home night," said Mollie, as she came in, "and they'll be here presently."

"All right, Mollie," said Miss Vernon, smiling. "I shan't stay more than a minute. I know I have come at an awkward time."

"She *would* come in, ma'am," said Mollie, as though she were not strong enough to thwart such a determined visitor.

As soon as the girl had gone Madge Vernon came across to Clare, very cheerfully and rather excitedly.

"Clare, are you coming?"

"Coming where?" asked Clare, trying to hide her agitation.

"To the demonstration," said Madge Vernon. "You know I told you all about it! It begins at eight. It will be immense fun, and after your window-smashing exploit you are one of us. Good Heavens, I think you have beaten us all. None of us have ever thought of breaking our own windows."

"It's my At Home night," said Clare.

"Oh, bother the At Home. Can't your husband look after his friends for once? I wanted you to join in this adventure. It would be your enrolment in the ranks, and it will do you a lot of good, in your present state of health."

"In any case——" said Clare.

"What?"

Clare smiled in a tragic way.

"I have received a previous invitation."

"Oh, drat the invitation."

"Of course I should have liked to come," said Clare, "but——"

Madge Vernon was impatient with her. "But what? I hate that word 'but.'"

"The spirit is willing but the flesh is weak," said Clare, speaking with a deeper significance than appeared in the words.

"There is no weakness about you. You have the courage of your convictions. Have you had the window mended yet?"

She laughed gaily and then listened with her head a little on one side to the sound of a bell ringing in the hall.

"That must be Herbert," said Clare. "I think you had better go."

"Yes, I think I had better," said Madge, laughing again. "If looks could kill——"

She went toward the door and opened it, but I stood on the threshold looking back.

"Won't you come? Eight o'clock, you know."

Clare smiled weakly.

"I am in great demand to-night."

The two women listened to Herbert's voice in the hall saying—

"Of course all the shops were shut."

"Oh, Lord!" said Madge, "I must skedaddle." She went out of the room hurriedly, leaving Clare alone.

And after a moment or two Clare spoke aloud, with her hands clasped upon her breast.

"I wonder if the Devil is tempting me tonight?" she said.

Then Herbert entered with two whisky bottles.

"I had to hunt all over the place," he said.

Then he saw that his wife was still in her afternoon frock, and his face flushed with anger.

"What, aren't you dressed *yet?*... I think you might show some respect for my wishes, Clare."

"I am going to dress now," said Clare, and she rose and went into the bedroom.

"Women are the very devil," said Herbert, unwrapping the whisky bottles.

While he was busy with this his mother came in, having changed her dress.

"Oh, I am glad you managed to get the whisky," she said.

"Of course nearly every blessed shop was shut," said Herbert. "They always are when I run out of everything. It's this Radical Government, with its beastly Acts."

Mrs. Heywood hesitated and then came across to her son and touched him on the arm.

"I think you had better come into the kitchen a moment, dear, and look after Mollie."

"She hasn't broken anything else, has she?" said Herbert anxiously.

"No, dear. But she has just cut her finger rather badly. She got in a temper with the sandwiches."

Herbert raised his hands to heaven.

"Why do these things always happen when Clare gives an At Home? I shall abolish these evenings altogether. They will drive me mad."

"Oh, they're very pleasant when they once begin," said Mrs. Heywood.

"I'm glad you think so, mother. I am damned if I do. I was only saying to Clare to-night——"

He stalked out of the room furiously.

Mrs. Heywood stood for a few moments staring at the carpet. Her lips moved and her worn old hands plucked at her skirt.

"Every time there is an At Home at this flat," she said, "I get another white hair."

She moved toward the door and went out of the room, so that it was left empty.

Outside in the street a piano-organ was playing a rag-time tune with a rattle of notes, and motor-cars were sounding their horns.

In this little drawing-room in Intellectual Mansions, Battersea Park, there was silence, except for those vague sounds from without. There was no sign here of Fate's presence, summoning a woman to her destiny. No angel stood with a flaming sword to bar the way to a woman with a wild heart. The little ormolu clock ticking on the mantel-shelf did not seem to be counting the moments of a tragic drama. It was a very commonplace little room, and the flamboyant chintz on the sofa and chairs gave it an air of cheerfulness, as though this were one of the happy homes of England.

Presently the bedroom door opened slowly, and Clare Heywood stood there looking into the drawing-room and listening. She was very pale, and was dressed in her outdoor things, as Gerald Bradshaw had asked her to dress, in her hat and cloak, so that she might slip out of the flat which he had called her prison.

She came further into the room, timidly, like a hare frightened by the distant baying of the hounds.

She raised her hands to her bosom, and spoke in a whisper:

"God forgive me!"

Then she crossed the floor, listened for a moment intently at the door, and slipped out. A moment or two later one's ears, if they had been listening, would have heard the front door shut.

Clare Heywood had escaped.

A little while later Mrs. Heywood, her mother-in-law, came into the room again and went over to the piano to open it and arrange the music.

"I do hope Clare is getting dressed," she said, speaking to herself.

Then Herbert came in, carrying a tray with decanter and glasses.

"Isn't Clare ready yet?" he asked.

"No, dear. She won't be long."

"I can't find the corkscrew," said Herbert, searching round for it, but failing to discover its whereabouts.

"Isn't it in the kitchen, dear?" asked Mrs. Heywood.

"Not unless Mollie has swallowed it. It's just the sort of thing she would do—out of sheer spite."

"Didn't you use it the other day to open a tin of sardines?" asked the old lady, cudgelling her brains.

"Did I?" said Herbert. "Oh, Lord, yes! I left it in the bathroom."

He went out of the room to find it.

Mrs. Heywood crossed over to the fire and swept up the grate.

"Clare is a very long time to-night," she said.

Then Mollie came in carrying a tray with some plates of sandwiches. One of her fingers was tied up with a rag.

"It's a good job the guests is late to-night," she remarked.

"Yes, we are all very behind-hand," said Mrs. Heywood.

Mollie dumped down the tray and gave vent to a little of her impertinent philosophy:

"I'll never give an At Home when I'm married. Blest if I do. Social 'ipocrisy, I call them."

Mrs. Heywood rebuked her sharply:

"We don't want your opinion, Mollie, thank you."

"I suppose I can *have* a few opinions, although I *am* in service," said Mollie. "There's plenty of time for thought even in the kitchen of a flat like this. I wonder domestic servants don't write novels. My word, what a revelation it would be! I've a good mind to write one of them serials in the *Daily Mail*."

"If I have any more of your impudence, Mollie——"

"It's not impudence," said Mollie. "It's aspirations."

The girl was silent when her master came into the room with the corkscrew.

"It wasn't in the bathroom," he explained. "I remember now, I used it for cleaning out my pipe."

"I could have told you that a long time ago, sir," said Mollie.

"Well, why the dickens didn't you?" asked Herbert.

"You never asked me, sir."

Mollie retired with the air of having scored a point.

"Well, as long as you've found it, dear," said Mrs. Heywood.

"Unfortunately, I broke the point. However, I daresay I can make it do."

He pulled one of the corks out of the whisky bottle and filled the decanter.

"Hasn't Clare finished dressing yet?" he said presently. "What on earth is she doing?"

"I expect she wants her blouse done up at the back," said Mrs. Heywood.

Herbert jerked up his head.

"And then she complains because I can't tie my own tie I Just like women."

He drew out another cork rather violently and said:

"Well, go and see after her, mother."

Mrs. Heywood went toward the bedroom door and called out in her silvery voice:

"Are you ready, dear?"

She listened for a moment, and called out again:

"Clare!"

Herbert poured some more whisky into the decanter.

"I expect she's reading one of those beastly pamphlets," he said.

Mrs. Heywood tapped at the bedroom door.

"Clare!"

"Go in, mother," said Herbert irritably.

"It's very strange!" said Mrs. Heywood in an anxious voice.

She went into the bedroom, and Herbert, who had been watching her, spilled some of the whisky, so that he muttered to himself:

"What with women and what with whisky——"

He did not finish his sentence, but stared in the direction of the bedroom as though suspecting something was wrong.

Mrs. Heywood came trembling out. She had a scared look.

"Oh, Herbert!"

Herbert was alarmed by the look on her face.

"Is Clare ill—or something?"

"She isn't there," said Mrs. Heywood.

The old lady was rather breathless.

"Not there!" said Herbert in a dazed way.

"She went in to dress a few minutes ago," said his mother.

Herbert stared at her. He was really very much afraid, but he spoke irritably:

"Well, she can't have gone up the chimney, can she? At least, I suppose not, though you never can tell nowadays."

He strode toward the bedroom door and called out:

"Clare!"

Then he went inside.

Mrs. Heywood stood watching the open door. She raised her hands up and then let them fall, and spoke in a hoarse kind of whisper:

"I think it has happened at last."

Herbert came out of the bedroom again. He looked pale, and had gloomy eyes.

"It's devilish queer!" he said.

Mother and son stood looking at each other, as though in the presence of tragedy.

"She must have gone out," said Mrs. Hey-wood.

"Gone out! What makes you think so?"

"She has taken her hat and cloak."

"How do you know?" asked Herbert.

"I looked in the wardrobe."

"Good Heavens! Where's she gone to?"

Mrs. Heywood's thin old hands clutched at the white lace upon her bosom.

"Herbert, I—I am afraid."

The man went deadly white. He stammered as he spoke:

"You don't mean that she is going to do something—foolish?"

"Something rash," said Mrs. Heywood mournfully.

Herbert had a sudden idea. It took away from his fear a little and made him angry.

"Perhaps she has gone round to church. If so, I will give her a piece of my mind when she comes back. It's outrageous! It's shameful."

There was the sound of a bell ringing through the hall, and the mother and son listened intently.

"Perhaps she *has* come back," said Herbert. "Perhaps she went to fetch some flowers." This idea seemed to soften him. His voice broke a little when he said: "Poor girl! I didn't mean to make such a fuss about them." "It isn't Clare," said Mrs. Heywood, shaking her head. "It's a visitor. I hear Mr. Atkinson Brown's voice."

Mr. Atkinson Brown's voice could be heard quite plainly in the hall:

"Well, Mollie, is your mistress quite well?" Herbert grasped his mother's arm and whispered to her excitedly:

"Mother, we must hide it from them."

"Yes," said Mrs. Heywood. "If the Atkinson Browns suspect anything it will be all over the neighborhood."

Herbert had a look of anguish in his eyes. "Good Heavens, yes. My reputation will be ruined."

Once again they heard Mr. Atkinson Brown's voice in the hall.

"I see we are the first to arrive," he said in a loud, cheery tone.

"Mother," whispered Herbert, "we must keep up appearances, at all costs."

"I'll try to, darling," said Mrs. Heywood, clasping his arm for a moment.

Herbert made a desperate effort to be hopeful.

"Clare is sure to be back in a few minutes. We're frightening ourselves for nothing.... I shall have something to say to her to-night when the guests are gone."

Mrs. Heywood's eyes filled with tears, and she looked at her son as though she knew that Clare would never come back.

"My poor boy!" she said.

"Play the game, mother," said Herbert. "For Heaven's sake play the game."

He had no sooner whispered these words than Mr. and Mrs. Atkinson Brown entered the room, having taken off their outdoor things. Mr. Brown was a tall, stout, heavily built man with a bald head and a great expanse of white waistcoat. His wife was a little bird-like woman in pink silk. They were both elaborately cheerful.

"Hulloh, Heywood, my boy!" said the elderly man.

"So delighted to come!" said Mrs. Atkinson Brown to Herbert's mother.

Herbert grasped the man's hand and wrung it warmly.

"Good of you to come. Devilish good."

"Glad to come," said Mr. Atkinson Brown. "Glad to come, my lad. How's the wife?"

"Yes," said Mrs. Atkinson Brown, glancing round the room. "Where's dear Clare?... Well, I hope."

Herbert tried to hide his extreme nervousness.

"Oh, tremendously fit, thanks. She'll be here in a minute or two."

Mrs. Heywood appeared less nervous than her son. Yet her voice trembled a little when she said:

"Do sit down, Mrs. Atkinson Brown."

She pulled a chair up, but the lady protested laughingly:

"Oh, not so near the fire. I can't afford to neglect my complexion at my time of life!"

Her husband was rubbing his hands in front of the fire. He had no complexion to spoil.

"Horrible weather for this time o' year," he said.

"Damnable," said Herbert, agreeing with him almost too cordially.

"Is dear Clare suited at present?" asked the lady.

"Well," said Mrs. Heywood, "we still have Mollie, but she is a great trouble—a very great trouble."

"Oh, the eternal servant problem!" said Mrs. Atkinson Brown. "I thought I had a perfect jewel, but I found her inebriated in the kitchen only yesterday."

Herbert was racking his brains for conversational subjects. He fell back on an old one. "Business going strong?"

"Business!" said Mr. Atkinson Brown. "My dear boy, business has been the very devil since this Radical Government has been in power."

"I am sure there has been a great deal of trouble in the world lately," said Mrs. Heywood.

"I'm sure I can't bear to read even the dear *Daily Mail*," said Mrs. Atkinson Brown.

"What with murders and revolutions and eloping vicars and suffragettes——"

"Those outrageous women ought to be whipped," said her husband. "Spoiled my game of golf last Saturday. Found 'Votes for Women' on the first green. Made me positively ill."

"I am glad dear Clare is so sensible," said Mrs. Atkinson Brown.

"Yes. Oh, quite so," said Mrs. Heywood, flushing a little.

"Oh, rather!" said Herbert.

"We domestic women are in the minority now," said Mrs. Atkinson Brown.

"The spirit of revolt is abroad, Herbert," said her husband. "Back to the Home is the only watchword which will save the country from these shameless hussies. Flog 'em back, I would. Thank God *our* wives have more sense."

"Yes, there's something in that," said Herbert.

Mrs. Atkinson Brown was gazing round the room curiously. She seemed to suspect something.

"You are sure dear Clare is quite well?" she asked. "No little trouble?"

"She is having a slight trouble with her back hair," said Herbert. "Won't lie down, you know."

He laughed loudly, as though he had made a good joke.

Mrs. Atkinson Brown half rose from her chair.

"Oh, let me go to the rescue of the dear thing!"

Herbert was terror-stricken.

"No—no! It was only my joke," he said eagerly. "She will be here in a minute. Do sit down."

Mrs. Heywood remembered her promise to "play the game."

"Won't you sing something, dear?" she said to her visitor.

"Oh, not so early in the evening," said the lady. "Besides, I have a most awful cold."

"Oh, I'm so sorry," said Herbert. "I am beastly sorry."

As he spoke the bell rang again, and Herbert went over to his mother and whispered to her:

"Do you think that is Clare? My God, this is awful!"

"Clare was not looking very well the other day when I saw her," said Mrs. Atkinson Brown. "I thought perhaps she was sickening for something."

"Oh, I assure you she was never better in her life," said Herbert.

"But you men are so unobservant. I am dying to see dear Clare, to ask her how she feels. Are you sure I can't be of any use to her?"

She rose again from her chair, and Herbert gave a beseeching look to his mother.

"Oh, quite sure, dear," said Mrs. Heywood. "*Do* sit down."

"Besides, you have such a frightful cold," said Herbert, with extreme anxiety. "*Do* keep closer to the fire."

Mrs. Atkinson Brown laughed a little curiously:

"You seem very anxious to keep me from dear Clare!"

This persistence annoyed her husband and he rebuked her sternly.

"Sit still, Beatrice, can't you? Don't you see that we have arrived a little early and that we have taken Clare unawares? Let the poor girl go on with her dressing."

"Don't bully me in other people's flats, Charles," said Mrs. Atkinson Brown. "I have enough of it at home."

Her husband was not to be quelled.

"Herbert and I can hardly hear ourselves speak," he growled, "you keep up such a clatter."

Mrs. Atkinson Brown flared up.

"I come out to get the chance of speaking a little. For eight years now I have been listening to your interminable monologues, and can't get a word in edgeways."

"Stuff and nonsense!" said her husband.

"Have you been married eight years already, my dear?" asked Mrs. Heywood in a tone of amiable surprise.

"Well, we are in our Eighth Year," said Mrs. Atkinson Brown.

Mrs. Heywood seemed startled.

"Oh, I see," she said thoughtfully.

"I assure you it seems longer," said the lady. "I suppose it's because Charles makes me so very tired sometimes."

Two other visitors now arrived. They were Mr. Hargreaves and his wife: the former a young man in immaculate evening clothes, with lofty manners; the latter a tall, thin, elegant, bored-looking woman, supercilious and snobbish.

Herbert went forward hurriedly to his new guests.

"How splendid of you to come! How are you, sir?"

"Oh, pretty troll-loll, thanks," said Mr. Hargreaves.

Herbert shook hands with Mrs. Hargreaves.

"How do you do?"

"We're rather late," said the lady, "but this is in an out-of-the-way neighborhood, is it not?"

"Oh, do you think so?" said Herbert. "I always considered Battersea Park very central."

Mrs. Hargreaves raised her eyebrows.

"It's having to get across the river that makes the journey so very tedious. I should die if I had to live across the river."

"There's something in what you say," said Herbert, anxious to agree with everybody. "I must apologize for dragging you all this way. Of course, you people in Mayfair——Won't you sit down?"

Mr. Hargreaves became a victim of mistaken identity, shaking hands with Mrs. Atkinson Brown.

"Mrs. Heywood, I presume. I must introduce myself."

Mrs. Hargreaves also greeted the other lady, under the same impression.

"Oh, how do you do? So delighted to make your acquaintance."

Mrs. Atkinson Brown was much amused, and laughed gaily.

"But I am *not* Mrs. Heywood. I cannot boast of such a handsome husband!"

"Oh, can't you, by Jove!" said Mr. Atkinson Brown, rather nettled by his wife's candor.

"Oh, I beg pardon," said Mr. Hargreaves. "Where *is* Mrs. Heywood?"

"Yes, where is Mrs. Heywood?" said his wife.

Herbert looked wildly at his mother.

"Where is she, mother? Do tell her to hurry up.

"Yes, dear," said Mrs. Heywood meekly. She moved uncertainly toward the bedroom door, and then hesitated: "Perhaps she will not be very long now."

"The fact is," said Herbert desperately, "she is not very well."

Mrs. Atkinson Brown was astounded.

"But you said she was perfectly well!"

"Did I?" said Herbert. "Oh, well, er—one has to say these things, you know. Polite fictions, eh?"

He laughed nervously.

"The fact is, she has a little headache. Hasn't she, mother?"

"Yes, dear," said Mrs. Heywood. "You know best."

Mrs. Atkinson Brown rose from her chair again.

"Oh, I will go and see how the poor dear feels. So bad of you to hide it from us."

"Oh, please sit down," said Herbert in a voice of anguish. "I assure you it is nothing very much. She will be in directly. Make yourself at home, Mrs. Hargreaves. This chair? Mother, show Mrs. Atkinson Brown Clare's latest photograph."

"Oh, yes!" said Mrs. Heywood. "It is an excellent likeness."

"But I want to see Clare herself!" said Mrs. Atkinson Brown plaintively.

"Sit down, Beatrice!" said her husband.

"Bully!" said Mrs. Atkinson Brown, sitting down with a flop.

Herbert addressed himself to Mr. Hargreaves.

"Draw up your chair, sir. You will have a cigar, I am sure."

He offered him one from a newly opened box. Mr. Hargreaves took one, smelled it, and then put it back.

"No, thanks," he said. "I will have one of my own, if I may. Sure the ladies don't mind?"

"Oh, they like it," said Herbert.

"We have to pretend to," said Mrs. Hargreaves.

"Well, if you don't, you ought to," said her husband. "It's a man's privilege."

Mrs. Hargreaves smiled icily.

"One of his many privileges."

"Will you have a cigarette, Mrs. Hargreaves?" said Herbert.

But Mr. Hargreaves interposed:

"Oh, I don't allow my wife to smoke. It's a beastly habit."

Mr. Atkinson Brown, who had accepted one of Herbert's cigars, but after some inquiry had also decided to smoke one of his own, applauded this sentiment with enthusiasm.

"Hear, hear! Hear, hear! Disgusting habit for women."

"Of course I agree with you," said Herbert. "Clare never smokes. But I don't lay down the law for other people's wives."

Mr. Hargreaves laughed.

"A very sound notion, Heywood. It takes all one's time to manage one's own, eh?"

"And then it is not always effective," said his wife. "Even the worm will turn."

Mr. Hargreaves answered his wife with a heavy retort:

"If it does I knock it on the head with a spade."

Mr. Atkinson Brown laughed loudly again. He seemed to like this man Hargreaves.

"Good epigram! By Jove, I must remember that!"

Herbert was on tenter-hooks when the conversation languished a little.

"Won't you sing a song, Mrs. Atkinson Brown? I am sure my friend, Mr. Hargreaves, will appreciate your voice."

"Oh, rather!" said Hargreaves. "Though I don't pretend to understand a note of music." Mrs. Atkinson Brown shook her head:

"I couldn't think of singing before our hostess appears."

The lady's husband seemed at last to have caught the spirit of her suspicion. He spoke in a hoarse whisper to his wife:

"Where the devil *is* the woman?"

Herbert Heywood realized that he was on the edge of a precipice. Not much longer could he hold on to this intolerable situation. He tried to speak cheerfully, but there was anguish in his voice when he said:

"Well, let's have a game of nap."

"Oh, Lord, no," said Hargreaves. "I only play nap on the way to a race. You don't sport a billiard table, do you?"

Herbert Heywood was embarrassed.

"Er—a billiard table?" He looked round the room as though he might discover a billiard table. "I'm afraid not."

"Don't be absurd, Edward," said Mrs. Hargreaves. "People don't play billiards on the wrong side of the river."

Conversation languished again, and Herbert was becoming desperate. He seized upon the sandwiches and handed them round.

"Won't anybody have a sandwich to pass the time away? Mrs. Hargreaves?"

Mrs. Hargreaves laughed in her supercilious way.

"It's rather early, isn't it?"

"Good Lord, no!" said Herbert. "I am sure you must be hungry. Let me beg of you—Mother, haven't you got any cake anywhere?"

"Yes, dear," said Mrs. Heywood. She, too, was suffering mental tortures.

"Atkinson Brown. You will have a sandwich," said Herbert.

He bent over to his visitor and spoke in a gloomy voice:

"Take one, for God's sake."

Atkinson Brown was startled.

"Yes! Yes! By all means," he said hastily. Herbert handed the sandwiches about rather wildly. "Mother, you will have one, won't you? Mrs. Atkinson Brown?... And one for me, eh?"

Mrs. Hargreaves eyed her host curiously.

"I hope your wife is not seriously unwell, Mr. Heywood."

Herbert was losing his nerve.

"Can't we talk of something else?" he said despairingly. "What is your handicap at golf?"

"My husband objects to my playing golf," said the lady.

"It takes women out of the home so much," said Hargreaves. "Play with the babies is my motto for women."

Mrs. Atkinson Brown shook her finger at him, and laughed in a shrill voice:

"But supposing they haven't got any babies?"

"They ought to have 'em," said Hargreaves.

It was Atkinson Brown who interrupted this interesting discussion, which promised to bring up the great problem of eugenics, so favored now as a drawing-room topic. He had been turning his sandwich this way and that, and he leaned forward to his host:

"Excuse me, Herbert, old man. There's something the matter with this sandwich."

"Something the matter with it?" asked Herbert anxiously.

"It's covered with red spots," said Atkinson Brown.

"Spots—what kind of spots?"

"Looks like blood," said Atkinson Brown, giving an uneasy guffaw. "Suppose there hasn't been a murder in this flat?"

All the guests leaned forward and gazed at the sandwich.

Herbert spoke in a tragic whisper to his mother:

"Mollie's finger!"

Then he explained the matter airily to the general company.

"Oh, it's a special kind of sandwich with the gravy outside. A new fad, you know."

"Oh, I see," said Atkinson Brown, much relieved. "Hadn't heard of it. Still, I think I'll have an ordinary one, if you don't mind."

Herbert was muttering little prayers remembered from his childhood.

"Mrs. Hargreaves," he said cajolingly, "I am sure you play. Won't you give us a little tune?"

"Well, if it won't disturb your wife," said the lady.

"Oh, I am sure it won't. She'll love to hear you."

He felt immensely grateful to this good-natured woman.

"Edward, get my music-roll," said Mrs. Hargreaves.

But Herbert had a horrible disappointment when Hargreaves said:

"By Jove! I believe I left it in the taxi. Yes, I am sure I did!"

Herbert put his hand up to his aching head and whispered his anguish:

"Oh, my God! Now how shall I mark time?"

"But I reminded you about it!" said Mrs. Hargreaves.

"Yes, I know. But you are always reminding me about something."

"Well, play something by heart," said Herbert in a pleading way. "Any old thing. The five-finger exercises."

"I am very out of practice," said Mrs. Hargreaves. "But still I will try."

Herbert breathed a prayer of thankfulness, and hurried to conduct the lady to the music-stool.

As he did so there was a noise outside the window. Newspaper men were shouting their sing-song: "Raid on the 'Ouse. Suffragette Outrage. Raid on the 'Ouse of Commins."

"What are the devils saying?" asked Hargreaves, trying to catch the words.

"Something about the Suffragettes," growled Atkinson Brown.

"I'm afraid it will give poor Clare a worse headache," said Mrs. Atkinson Brown.

Mrs. Heywood tried to be reassuring:

"Oh, I don't think so."

At that moment there was a loud ring at the bell. The sound was so prolonged that it startled the company.

Herbert listened intently and then whispered to his mother:

"That must be Clare!"

"Oh, if it is only Clare!" said Mrs. Heywood. When Mrs. Hargreaves had struck a few soft chords on the piano there was the sound of voices speaking loudly in the hall. Everybody listened, surprised at the interruption. Mollie's voice could be heard quite clearly.

"I told you it was our At Home night, Miss Vernon."

"I can't help that."

The drawing-room door opened, *sans ceremonie*, and Madge Vernon came in. Her face was flushed, and she had sparkling eyes. She stood in the doorway looking at the company with a smile, as though immensely amused by some joke of her own.

"I'm sorry to interrupt you good people," she said very cheerfully, "but I have come on urgent business, which brooks no delay, as they say in melodrama."

Mrs. Heywood gazed at her with frightened eyes.

"My dear!... What has happened?"

"What's the matter?" said Herbert, turning very pale.

"Oh, it's nothing to be alarmed at," said Madge Vernon. "It's about your wife."

"My wife?"

"About Clare?" exclaimed Mrs. Atkinson Brown.

Mrs. Hargreaves craned her head forward, like a bird reaching for its seed.

"I wonder—" she said.

Madge Vernon grinned at them all.

"It'll be in the papers to-morrow, so you are all bound to know. Besides, why keep it a secret? It's a thing to be proud of!"

"Proud of what?" asked Herbert in a frenzied tone of voice.

Madge Vernon enjoyed the drama of her announcement.

"Clare has been arrested in a demonstration outside the House to-night."

"Arrested!"

The awful word was spoken almost simultaneously by all the company in that drawingroom of Intellectual Mansions, S. W.

"She's quite safe," said Madge Vernon calmly. "I've come to ask you to bail her out."

Herbert's guests rose and looked at him in profound astonishment and indignation.

"But you told us—" cried Mrs. Atkinson Brown.

Herbert Heywood gave a queer groan of anger and horror.

"Bail her out!... Oh, my God!"

He sank down into his chair and held his head in his hands.

CHAPTER III

Herbert Heywood was in the depths of an arm-chair reading the paper. Mrs. Heywood was on the other side of the fireplace with a book on her lap. But she was dozing over it, and her head nodded on to her chest. Herbert turned over the leaves of the paper and then studied the advertisements. He had a look of extreme boredom. Every now and then he yawned quietly and lengthily. At last he let the paper fall on to the floor, and uttered his thoughts aloud, so that his mother was awakened.

"Did you say anything, Herbert?" said the old lady.

"Nothing, mother, except that I am bored stiff."

He went over to the piano and played "God Save the King" with one finger, in a doleful way.

Mrs. Heywood glanced over her spectacles at him.

"Would you like a game of cribbage, dear?"

"No, thanks, mother," said Herbert hastily. "Not in the afternoon."

Mrs. Heywood listened to his fumbling notes for a moment and then spoke again.

"Won't you go out for a walk? It would do you good, Herbert."

"Think so?" said Herbert bitterly; without accepting the suggestion, he played "Three Blind Mice," also with one finger. It sounded more melancholy than "God Save the King."

"I don't like to see you moping indoors on a bright day like this," said Mrs. Heywood. "Take a brisk walk round the Park. It would cheer you up."

Herbert resented the idea fiercely.

"A long walk in Battersea Park would make a pessimist of a laughing hyena."

Mrs. Heywood was silent for some time, but then she made a last effort.

"Well, go and see a friend, dear. The Atkinson Browns, for instance."

"They do nothing but nag at each other," said Herbert. "And Atkinson Brown hasn't as much brains as a Teddy Bear. Besides, he's become friendly with that fellow Hargreaves, and I'm not going to take the risk of meeting a man who turned me out of my job."

Mrs. Heywood became agitated.

"Are you sure of that, Herbert? I can't think he could have been so malicious, after coming here and eating your salt, as it were. What was his reason?"

"He made no disguise of it," said Herbert bitterly. "I saw his letter to my chief. Said that it was quite impossible to employ a man who was mixed up with the militant Suffragettes. Damned liar!"

"Good Heavens!" said Mrs. Heywood.

"Of course it was all due to that ghastly evening when Clare got arrested. She knows that well enough."

"Well, dear," said Mrs. Heywood, "she has tried to make amends. The shock of your losing your place has made her much more gentle and loving. It has brought back all her loyalty to you, Herbert."

"Loyalty!" said Herbert. "Where is she now, I should like to know?"

"She is gone to some committee meeting."

"She's always got a committee meeting," said Herbert angrily, kicking the hassock.

"She joins a new committee for some kind of social reform nonsense every blessed day."

"Well, it keeps her busy, dear," said Mrs. Heywood gently. "Besides, it is not all committee work. Since she has been visiting the poor and helping in the slums she has been ever so much better in health and spirits."

"Yes, but where the devil do I come in?" asked Herbert.

"Don't you think you might go out, dear? Just for a little while?"

"I don't *want* to go out, mother," said Herbert with suppressed heat.

"Very well, dear."

Herbert stood in front of the fireplace and rattled the keys in his pocket moodily.

"What's the good of toiling to keep a home together if one's wife abandons her husband's society on every possible pretext? A home! This place is just a receiving office for begging letters and notices for committees and subcommittees."

Mrs. Heywood sighed.

"It might have been worse, Herbert."

"As far as I'm concerned, it couldn't be worse. I'm the most miserable wretch in London. Without a job and without a wife."

"You'll get a place all right, dear. You have the promise of one already. And you know Clare's health was in a very queer state before Miss Vernon made her take an interest in helping other people. I was seriously alarmed about her."

"What about me?" asked Herbert. "No one troubles to get alarmed about me."

"Are you unwell, dear?" said Mrs. Hey-wood anxiously.

"Of course I'm unwell."

"Darling!" said Mrs. Heywood, still more anxiously.

"Oh, there's nothing the matter with me from a physical point of view. But mentally and morally I'm a demnition wreck."

"Aren't you taking your iron pills regularly?" said his mother.

"Pills! As if pills could cure melancholia!" Mrs. Heywood was aghast at that dreadful word.

"Good Heavens, dear!"

"I'm on the verge of a nervous breakdown," said Herbert.

"Oh, Herbert," cried his mother, "I hope not!"

"I'm working up to a horrible crisis," said Herbert.

"What are your symptoms? How do you feel?" asked his mother.

"I feel like smashing things," said Herbert savagely.

He sat down at the piano again and played "We Won't Go Home Till Morning," but missed his note, and banged on to the wrong one in a temper.

"There goes a note, anyhow. Thank goodness for that!"

At that moment Mollie came in holding a silver tray with a pile of letters.

"The post, sir."

"Well, something to break the infernal monotony," said Herbert with a sigh of relief.

He took up the letters and examined them.

"Life is a bit flat, sir," said Mollie, "since we gave up having At Homes."

"Hold your tongue," said Herbert.

Mollie tossed her head and muttered an impertinent sentence as she left the room.

"Can't even open my mouth without somebody jumping down my throat. I will break that girl's neck one of these days," said Herbert.

He went through the letters and read out the names on them.

"Mrs. Herbert Heywood, *Mrs.* Herbert Heywood, Mrs. Herbert Heywood, Mrs. Herbert—Why, every jack one is for Mrs. Herbert Heywood! Nobody writes to me, of course. No one cares a damn about *me*."

"Your mother cares, Herbert," said the old lady.

"I shall take to drink—or the devil," said Herbert, and he added thoughtfully, "I wonder which is the most fun?"

"Herbert, dear!" cried his mother, "don't say such awful things."

"The worst of it is," said Herbert bitterly, "they're both so beastly expensive."

There was the noise of a latchkey in the hall, and Mrs. Heywood gave a little cry.

"There's Clare!"

"Think so?" said Herbert, listening.

From the hall came the sound of Clare's voice singing a merry tune.

"She's in a cheerful mood, anyhow," said Mrs. Heywood, smiling.

Herbert answered her gloomily.

"Horribly cheerful."

The mother and son looked toward the door as Clare came in. There was a noticeable change in her appearance since the evening At Home. There was more color in her cheeks and the wistfulness had gone out of her eyes. She was brisk, keen and bright.

"Well, mother," she said, "been having a nap?"

"Oh, no, dear," said the old lady, who never admitted that she made a habit of naps.

"Hulloh, Herbert," said Clare. "Have you got that new post yet?"

"No," said Herbert. "And I don't expect I shall get it."

"Oh, yes, you will, dear old boy. Don't you worry! Have you been home long?"

"Seems like a lifetime."

Clare laughed.

"Not so long as that, surely?"

She came forward to him and put her arm about his neck, and offered him her cheek. He looked at it doubtfully for a moment and then kissed her in a "distant" manner.

"I'm frightfully busy, old boy," said Clare. "I just have a few minutes and then I shall have to dash off again."

"Dash off where?" asked Herbert, with signs of extreme irritation. "Dash it all, surely you aren't going out again?"

"Only round the corner," said Clare quietly. "I have got to look into the case of a poor creature who is making match-boxes. Goodness knows how many for a farthing! And yet she's so cheerful and plucky that it does one good to see her. Oh, it kills one's own selfishness, Herbert."

"Well, why worry about her, then, if she's so pleased with herself?"

"She's plucky," said Clare, "but she's starving. It's a bad case of sweated labor."

"Sweated humbug," said Herbert. "What am I going to do all the evening, I should like to know? Sit here alone?"

"I don't suppose I shall be long," said Clare. "Besides, there's mother."

"Yes, there's mother," said Herbert. "But when a man's married he wants his wife."

Clare was now busy looking over her letters.

"Can't you go to the club?" she asked.

"I'm dead sick of the club. That boiled-shirt Bohemianism is the biggest rot in the world."

"Take mother to the theatre," said Clare cheerfully.

"The theatre bores me stiff. These modern plays set one's nerves on edge."

"Well, haven't you got a decent novel or anything?" said Clare, reading one of her letters.

"A decent novel! There's no such thing nowadays, and they give me the hump."

Clare was reading another letter with absorbed interest, but she listened with half an ear, as it were, to her husband.

"Play mother a game of cribbage, then," she said.

"Look here, Clare," said Herbert furiously, "I shall begin to throw things about in a minute."

"Don't get hysterical, Herbert," said Clare calmly. "Especially as I have got some good news for you."

As she spoke these words she looked across a Demonstration to him with a curious smile and added: "A big surprise, Herbert!"

"A surprise?" said Herbert with sarcasm. "Have you discovered another widow in distress?"

"Well, I have," said Clare, "but it's not that."

Mrs. Heywood glanced from her son to her daughter-in-law, and seemed to imagine that she might be disturbing an intimate conversation.

"I will be back in a minute. I won't disturb you two dears," she said, as she left the room quietly.

"You won't disturb us, mother," said Clare.

But the old lady smiled and said, "I won't be long."

"Are you going to get arrested again?" asked Herbert. "Do you want me to bail you out? Because by the Lord, I won't!"

"Oh, that was quite an accident," said Clare, laughing. "Besides, I gave you my word to abstain from the militant movement, and you can't say I have broken the pledge."

"You have broken a good many other things."

"What kind of things?" asked Clare. "You aren't alluding to that window again, are you?"

"You have broken my illusions on married life," said Herbert, with tragic emphasis.

"Ah," said Clare, "that is 'the Great Illusion,' by the Angel in the House."

"You have broken my ideals of womanhood."

"They were false ideals, Herbert," said Clare very quietly. "It was only a plaster ideal which broke. The real woman is of flesh and blood. The real woman is so much better than the sham. Don't you think so?"

"It depends on what you call sham," said Herbert.

"I was a sham until that plaster image of me broke. I indulged in sham sentiment, sham emotion, sham thoughts. Look at me now, since I went outside these four walls and faced the facts of life, and saw other people's misery besides my own, and the happiness of people with so much more to bear than I had. Look into my eyes, Herbert."

She smiled at him tenderly, alluringly. "What's the good?" said Herbert.

"Do you see a weary soul looking out?"

Herbert looked into his wife's eyes for a moment and then stared down at the carpet.

"I used to see love looking out," he said.

"It's looking out now," said Clare. "Love of life instead of discontent. Love of this great throbbing human nature, with so much to be put right. Love of poor people, and little children, and brave hearts. Madge Vernon taught me that, for she has a soul bigger than the suffrage, and ideals that go beyond the vote. I have blown the cobwebs out of my eyes, Herbert. I see straight."

"How about *me?*" asked Herbert. "That's what I want to know. Where do I come in?"

"Oh, you come in all right!" said Clare. "You are a part of life and have a big share of my love."

"I don't want to be shared up, thanks," said Herbert.

She stroked his hand.

"I love you much better now that I see you with this new straight vision of mine. At any rate I love what is real in you and not what is sham. And I have learned the duties of love, Herbert. I believe I am a better wife to you. I think I have learned the meaning of marriage, and of married love."

She spoke with a touch of emotion, and there was a thrill in her voice.

"You are in love with your social work and your whining beggars, not with me. You are getting farther and farther away from me. You leave me alone; I come back to a neglected home."

"Why, Mollie and mother look after it beautifully," said Clare very cheerfully.

Herbert gave expression to his grievances.

"I come home and ask, 'Where is Clare?' and get the eternal answer, 'Clare is out.' I am an abandoned husband, and by Heaven I won't stand it. I will——"

"What, Herbert?" said Clare, smiling up at him. "Don't do anything rash, old boy."

"I—have a good mind to make love to somebody else's wife. But they're all so beastly ugly!"

"Perhaps somebody else's wife won't respond," said Clare. "Some women are very cold."

"I'll take to drink. I have already given mother full warning."

"I am sure it will disagree with you, dear," said Clare.

"You scoff at me," said Herbert passionately. "I think we had better live apart."

"You would get even more bored than before. Dear old boy. *Do* be reasonable. *Do* cultivate a sense of humor."

"This is not a farce," said Herbert. "It's a horrible tragedy."

"Take up a hobby or something," said Clare. "Golf—or fretwork."

Herbert was furious.

"Fretwork! Is that a joke or an insult?"

"It was only a suggestion!" said Clare. Herbert jumped up from his chair.

"I had better go and drown myself straight away..."?

He turned at the door, and gave a tragic look at his wife. "Good-by."

Clare smiled at him.

"Won't you kiss me before you go?"

"I will take my pipe," said Herbert, coming back to the mantelshelf. "It's my only friend."

"It will go out in the water," said Clare. "Besides, Herbert, don't you want to hear my good news? My big surprise?"

"No," said Herbert. "Nothing you could say or do could surprise me now. If mother wants me I shall be in the study for the rest of the evening."

"But I thought you were going to the river?", said Clare teasingly.

Herbert was not to be amused.

"I suppose you think you're funny? I don't," he said.

Then he went out and slammed the door. Clare was left alone, and there was a smile about her lips.

"Poor old Herbert," she said. "I think he will have the surprise of his life."

She laughed quietly to herself, and then looked up and listened as she heard a slight noise. She stood up with a sudden look of anger as she saw Gerald Bradshaw gazing at her through the open French windows.

The man spoke to her in his soft, silky voice.

"Clare, why are you so cruel to me? I have been ill because of your heartlessness."

Clare answered him sternly.

"I thought I had got rid of you. Have you come back to plague me?"

"I tried to forget you," said Gerald Bradshaw. "I went as far as Italy to forget you. I made love to many women to forget you. But I have come back. And I shall always come back, because you are my mate and I cannot live without you."

Clare's voice rang out in the room.

"God ought not to let you live. Every word you speak is a lie. You are a thief of women's honor. Get away from my window, because your very breath is poison."

The man was astonished, a little scared. "You did not speak like that once, Clare. You let me hold your hand. You trembled when I leaned toward you."

"I was ill and weak," said Clare, "and you tried to tempt my weakness. I was blind and did not see the evil in you. But now I am well and strong, and my eyes are opened to the truth of things. If you don't go I will call my husband and he will throw you over that balcony at one word from me."

Gerald Bradshaw laughed scoffingly.

"Your husband! I could kill him between my thumb and forefinger."

"He is strong because he is good," said Clare. "I will call him now."

She went quickly toward the bell.

"You needn't call him," said Gerald Bradshaw. "I would dislike to hurt the little man."

"You are going?" asked Clare.

"Yes, I am going," said the man, "because something has changed in you."

Clare gave a cheerful little laugh.

"You are right."

"I see that now. I have lost my spell over you. Something has broken."

"Are you going," said Clare sternly, "or shall I call my man?"

"I am going, Clare," said the man at the window. "I am going to find another mate. She and I will talk evil of you, and hate you, as I hate you now. Farewell, foolish one!" He withdrew from the window, and instantly Clare rushed to it, shut it and bolted it. Then she pulled down the blind, and stood, panting, with her back to it and her arms outstretched.

"God be praised!" she said. "He has gone out of my life. I am a clean woman again." At that moment Mrs. Heywood entered. "Must you go out again, Clare?" said the old lady.

"Only for a little while, mother," said Clare, a little breathless after her emotion.

"Is anything the matter, dear?" said Mrs. Heywood. "You look rather flustered."

"Oh, nothing is the matter!" said Clare. "Only I am very happy."

Mrs. Heywood smiled at her.

"It makes me happy to see you so well and bright," she said.

"I don't get on your nerves so much, eh, mother?"

She laughed quietly.

"Well, I must go and tidy my hair."

She moved toward the bedroom, but stopped to pack up her letters.

"I am so sorry you have to go out," said the old lady.

"I shan't be more than a few minutes," said Clare. "But I must go. Besides, after this I am going to *give* up some of my visiting work."

"Give it up, dear?"

"Yes. One must be moderate even in district visiting."

She went into the bedroom, but left the door open so that she could hear her mother.

"Clare!" said the old lady.

"Yes, mother."

"What is that surprise you were going to give us?"

"Surprise, mother?"

"Yes," said Mrs. Heywood. "The good news?"

"Oh, yes, I forgot," said Clare. "Come in and I will tell you."

Mrs. Heywood went into the bedroom. Outside, in the street, a man with a fiddle was playing the "Intermezzo." Presently both women came out. Clare was smiling, with her arm round Mrs. Heywood's neck. Mrs. Heywood was wiping her eyes as though crying a little.

"Cheer up," said Clare. "It's nothing to cry about."

"I am crying because I am so glad," said Mrs. Heywood.

"Well, that's a funny thing to do," said Clare, laughing gaily. "Now I must run away. You won't let Herbert drown himself, will you?"

"No, dear," said Mrs. Heywood, wiping her eyes.

"Who would have thought it!" said Mrs.

Heywood, speaking to herself as her daughter-in-law left the room.

She went over to the mantelpiece and took up her son's photograph and kissed it. Then she went to the door and stood out in the hall and called in a sweet old woman's voice:

"Herbert! Herbert, dear!"

"Are you calling, mother?" answered Herbert from another room.

"Yes," said Mrs. Heywood. "I want you."

"I don't feel a bit like cribbage, mother,'" said Herbert.

"I don't want you to play cribbage to-night," said the old lady. "I have something to say to you."

"Has Clare gone?" asked Herbert, still calling from the other room.

"Yes," said Mrs. Heywood. "But she won't be long."

"Oh, all right. I'll be along in a moment."

Mrs. Heywood went back into the room and waited for her son eagerly. Presently he came in with a pipe in his hand and book under his arm. He had changed into a shabby old jacket, and was in carpet slippers.

"What's the matter, mother?" he asked.

"There's nothing the matter," said the old lady; then she became very excited, and raised her hands and cried out:

"At least, everything is the matter. It's the only thing that matters! ... Oh, Herbert!"

She laughed and cried at the same time so that her son was alarmed and stared at her in amazement.

"You aren't ill, are you?" he said. "Shall I send for a doctor?"

Mrs. Heywood shook her trembling old head.

"I'm quite well. I never felt so well."

"You had better sit down, mother," said Herbert.

He took her hand and led her to a chair.

"What's up, eh, old lady? Mollie hasn't run away, has she?"

The old lady took his hand and fondled it.

"Herbert, my son, I've wonderful news for you."

"News?" said Herbert. "Did you find it in the evening paper?"

"It's going to make a lot of difference to us all," said Mrs. Heywood. "No more cribbage, Herbert!"

"Thank heaven for that!" said Herbert.

"And not so much social work for Clare."

"Well, let's be thankful for small mercies," said Herbert.

"Bend your head down and let me whisper to you," said Mrs. Heywood.

She put her hands up to his head, and drew it down, and whispered something into his ears.

It was something which astounded him.

He started back and said "No!" as though he had heard something quite incredible. Then he spoke in a whisper:

"By Jove!... Is that a fact?"

"It's the best fact that ever was, Herbert," said the old lady.

"Yes... it will make a bit of a difference," said Herbert thoughtfully.

Mrs. Heywood clasped her son's arm. There was a tremulous light in her eyes and a great emotion in her voice.

"Herbert, I am an old woman and your mother. Sit down and let me talk to you as I did in the old days when you were my small boy before a nursery fire."

Herbert smiled at her; all the gloom had left his face.

"All right, mother.... By Jove, and I never guessed. And yet I ought to have guessed. Things have been—different—lately."

He sat down on a hassock near the old lady with his knees tucked up. She sat down, too, and stretched out a trembling hand to touch his hair.

"Once upon a time, Herbert, there was a young man and a young woman who loved each other very dearly."

Herbert looked up and smiled at her.

"Are you sure, mother?"

"Perfectly sure. Then they married."

"And lived happily ever after? I bet they didn't!"

"No, not quite happily, because this is different from the fairy tales. ... After a time the husband began to think too much about his work, while the wife stayed at home and thought too much about herself."

"It's a stale old yarn," said Herbert. "What happened then?"

"By degrees the wife began to think she hated her husband, because although he gave her little luxuries and pretty clothes, and all the things that pleased *him*, he never gave her the thing *she* wanted."

"What was that?" asked Herbert.

"It was a magic charm to make her forget herself."

"Well, magic charms aren't easy to find," said Herbert.

"No.... But at last she went out to find it herself. And while she was away the husband came home and missed her."

"Poor devil!" said Herbert. "Of course he did."

"Being a man," said Mrs. Heywood, giving a queer little laugh, "he stayed at home more than he used to do, and then complained that he was left too much alone. Just like his wife had complained."

"Well, hang it all," said Herbert, "she ought to have stayed with him."

"But then she wouldn't have found the magic charm," said Mrs. Heywood. "Don't you see?... And she would have withered and withered away until there was nothing left of her, and the husband would have been quite alone—forever."

"Think so?" said Herbert very thoughtfully. "D'you think it would have been as bad as that?"

"Yes," said Mrs. Heywood. "I'm sure of it."

"Well, what did happen?" asked Herbert. "Did she find the magic charm? It wasn't a widow in distress, was it? Or Social Reform humbug?"

"No," said Mrs. Heywood; "that gave her a new interest in life because it helped her to forget herself, some of her own little worries, some of her brooding thoughts. But a good fairy who was looking after her worked another kind of magic.... Herbert I It's the best magic for unhappy women and unhappy homes, and it has been worked for you. Oh, my dear, you ought to be very thankful."

"Yes," said Herbert, scratching his head. "Yes, I suppose so. But what's the moral of the tale, mother? I'm hanged if I see."

Mrs. Heywood put her hand on her son's shoulder, as he sat on the hassock by her chair.

"It's a moral told by an old woman who watched these two from the very beginning. A husband mustn't expect his wife to stay at home for ever. The home isn't big enough, Herbert. There's the great world outside calling to her, calling, calling. The walls of a little fiat like this are too narrow for the spirit and heart. If he keeps her there she either pines and dies, or else——"

"What?" asked Herbert.

"Escapes, my dear," said the old lady very solemnly.

Herbert drew a deep, quivering breath.

"Then," said Mrs. Heywood, "nothing in the world can call her back—except——"

"Except what?"

"A little child."

Herbert got up from the hassock and clasped the mantelshelf, and spoke in a low, humble, grateful voice.

"Thank God, Clare has been called back!" he said.

Mrs. Heywood rose from her chair also, and caught hold of her son's sleeve.

"Yes," she said, "yes. But even now she will want to spread her wings a little. She must take short flights, Herbert, even now. She must wing her way out to the big world at times. You will remember that, won't you?"

"I'll try to remember," said Herbert. He bent his head over his hands on the mantelshelf. "I've been selfish," he said. "Blinded with selfishness and self-conceit. God forgive me."

"Perhaps we have all been a little selfish," said Mrs. Heywood quietly. "But we shall have some one else to think about now. A new life, Herbert. A new life is coming to us all!"

"Hush!" said Herbert. "Here's Clare."

The mother and son stood listening to the voice of Clare singing in the hall. She was singing the old nursery rhyme of—

"Sing a song of sixpence,
A pocket-full of rye,
Four and twenty blackbirds
Baked in a pie,
When the pie was opened——"

Mrs. Heywood smiled into her son's eyes.

"I think I've left my spectacles in the other room," she said. She went out into the hall, leaving her son alone.

And Herbert stood with his head raised, looking toward the door, eagerly, like a lover waiting for his bride.

Then Clare came in. There was a smile about her lips, and she spoke cheerfully.

"Well, you see I wasn't long."

Herbert strode toward her and took her hands and raised them to his lips.

"Clare, sweetheart! Is it true? Have you been called back to me?"

Clare put her forehead down against his chest.

"I never went very far away," she said.

Presently Herbert spoke again with great cheerfulness.

"I say, Clare. It's a funny thing!"

"What's a funny thing?" asked Clare, smiling at him.

"Why, I was reading the advertisements in the paper to-night—"

"Were *they* funny?" asked Clare.

"No," said Herbert, "but I saw something that would just suit us."

He went over to a side-table and picked up the newspaper. Sitting on the edge of the table, he read out an advertisement.

"Here it is.... 'Chelsea—Semi-detached house, dining-room, drawing-room, three bedrooms, and a large nursery. Shed for bicycle or perambulator.'"

Clare laughed happily.

"Well, we might have both!" she said.

Herbert dropped the paper, came over to his wife, and kissed her hands again.

THE END

Milton Keynes UK
Ingram Content Group UK Ltd.
UKHW021125030424
440506UK00009B/1198